Hatching Magic

Other books by Ann Downer

The Spellkey
The Glass Salamander
The Books of the Keepers

ANN DOWNER

Hatching Magic

ATHENEUM BOOKS FOR YOUNG READERS
New York London Toronto Sydney Singapore

Atheneum Books for Young Readers
An imprint of Simon & Schuster Children's Publishing Division
1230 Avenue of the Americas
New York, New York 10020

Book design by Ann Sullivan
The text of this book is set in Centaur MT.

Printed in the United States of America

6 8 10 9 7 5

Library of Congress Cataloging-in-Publication Data
Downer, Ann, 1960–
Hatching magic / by Ann Downer.
p. cm.
Summary: When a thirteenth-century wizard confronts twenty-first-century Boston while seeking his pet dragon, he is followed by a rival wizard and a very unhappy demon, but eleven-year-old Theodora Oglethorpe may hold the secret to setting everything right.
ISBN 0-689-83400-4
[1. Wizards—Fiction. 2. Dragons—Fiction. 3. Time travel—Fiction. 4. Magic—Fiction. 5. Fathers and daughters—Fiction. 6. Nannies—Fiction.] I. Title.
PZ7.D7575 Wi 2003
[Fic]—dc21 00-56570

For Ed, with love, for always believing Wycca would make her way out of my imagination and onto the page with her scales unruffled and magic intact, and For Bennet, who generously shared his early months of life with the completion of this book, with very little complaint.

Contents

Hatching
Magic

I

A Rabbit Hole through Time

LIKE A CAT that hides under the barn to have her kittens, a wyvern mother-to-be likes a nice, private spot to lay her egg.

Wycca had inspected several chambers around the castle and rejected them all. This one was unpleasantly hot, that one, drafty; this one smelled of mildew, that one was too close to the privies; and yet another was next to the bedchamber of the king's steward, who snored.

Wycca sighed. It was all very trying to a wyvern in a delicate predicament.

She shifted on her perch on the castle ramparts, doing her best to look inconspicuous while she enjoyed her afternoon bask in the sun. The courtiers in the garden below were gathered around a lute player by the fountain and didn't seem to notice the extra gargoyle high overhead.

Wycca flexed her claws and began to give herself a leisurely manicure, cat fashion. She fit in well among the ramparts, being about the size of the stone gargoyle waterspouts. She was a small, four-legged dragon with a neat, slender head and an eagle's beak. No matter what old bestiaries and modern dictionaries have to say on the matter, wyverns do have forelimbs as well as hindlimbs, and a set of powerful, membranous flapping wings, like those of a bat. Wyverns are the most catlike of the dragons in their agility, intelligence, temperament, and vanity, and like a cat, Wycca had slitted, feline eyes, retractable claws, and a deep, melodious purr.

This morning's nest-hunting had begun promisingly. Hidden behind a tapestry at the back of the queen's chapel, Wycca had discovered a small chest full of prayer books half eaten by bookworms. Their pages would make a fine, soft nest, and the little chapel itself was warm, dry, quiet, and unused, the humans having long ago abandoned it to mice and bats.

She had been happily planning the lining of the nest—fresh cobwebs, down from young owls, perhaps a few golden hairs from the princess's hairbrush—when the men came in and began to haul out the broken furniture.

The old king had recently remarried, and his new queen was young, French, and devout. Someone had remembered the neglected chapel. It was to be swept out, given a fresh coat of whitewash, and fumigated. The promising chest was the first thing to go on the bonfire. Wycca hid in the choir loft and watched the monks' beautifully carved pews turn to smoke. She would have to start her search all over again.

There was an easier way. Her master, Gideon, was the king's own wizard, and his chambers were warm and dry and quiet. Gideon knew she was about to lay an egg. He had placed a folding screen around her favorite sleeping place and now gave her a dose of swan-liver oil after dinner. It would have been simple to shred a cushion or two, line the heap with a few mouse whiskers and moth wings, and be done with it.

But Wycca had her dignity. Nests were not provided. They had to be sought with difficulty, discovered by cleverness, and kept hidden from everyone—especially wizards. Even her own wizard.

The sun went behind a cloud, signaling that basking time had come to an end. Wycca bestirred herself. The egg made her ungainly, and Wycca could feel it shift as she struggled to her feet. She was overcome by a powerful urge, to dig, to tear something up—she had to make her nest. But where?

She fled (if you can call a swift waddle fleeing) to the back of the garden by the crumbling wall that was all that remained of a much older castle, leveled in a long-ago siege. She was venting some of her nest-building urges on the ground, clawing out a deep wallow among the melons, when she found it.

At first she thought she had dug through to the wall, but it wasn't stone. It wasn't earth, either, or fire or ice or air, or any other substance she knew—except one. Wycca sat back on her haunches and snorted in surprise.

It felt like magic.

Her master's magic was kept tightly corked in bottles and jars, to be let out only when the moon was waning and the wind was out of the right quarter, and then only in small amounts, ground up in a mortar with barley wine and ashes until it was the right strength for repelling demons or fetching wyverns.

But this magic had never known the inside of a jar. It was wild and strong and willful. It yawned suddenly, so that it was bigger than the largest melon, bigger than Wycca. The center of it wavered like summer heat on tiled rooftops, only cool and silver and humming faintly. It pulled at her, like the tug of the moon on the sea.

Suddenly, Wycca knew where she would build her nest.

She stretched out her neck slowly until the very tip of her beak broke the surface of the shimmering wildness. There was a ripple and a sound like a harp string being plucked, and in that heartbeat Wycca was instantly and completely Elsewhere. There was nothing in the melon patch but some tangled melon vines and a spot of darker, clawed earth.

When Wycca didn't show up for dinner, Gideon didn't think much of it. It was her habit to dawdle when he called, so that her appearance, when she finally made it, would seem like her own idea. After all, she seemed to say, curling up on the rug before the fire, only dogs and other witless creatures came when you whistled.

But when it began to grow dark and she still had not returned, Gideon began to worry. He hoped the silly creature hadn't gotten wedged into a tight spot somewhere down in the crypt—or, worse, the dungeon. But most of all, he hoped no one had taken her. Even a fetched wyvern—one summoned by spellcraft and given a golden collar and a Name—is still a magical creature. Wycca could be a powerful weapon against her wizard if she fell into the hands of his enemies.

Someone like Kobold, for instance.

Gideon and Kobold had grown up together, and when they turned sixteen, they had been apprenticed to the king's wizard. Both young men had won favor at court, and when the old wizard had retired to the country to raise bees, both of them vied for the coveted position of Sorcerer Royal. In the end, the king awarded Gideon the title and the wand, and Kobold had to hire himself out as an itinerant wizard, riding a circuit between various third earls and aging warlords. Unfortunately, Kobold had a lot of time left over to nurse his grudge and to sharpen his skills at summoning the minor demons. These he sent to the castle to spy on Gideon. If Wycca was missing, Gideon thought to himself, Kobold would learn about it soon enough. And if he could find a way to wreak his revenge, he would.

Gideon threw on his cloak and went out to look for Wycca. He started by checking all her favorite hiding places. She wasn't drinking buttermilk in the dairy or napping beside the fire in the laundry, where the linens were hung to dry. She wasn't hunting frogs among the lilies in the moat or teasing the high-strung falcons in their mews. She wasn't taking a dust bath on the jousting grounds.

He was lying flat on his stomach trying to get a good look under the dovecote when he heard a honeyed voice say, "Have you lost something, Gideon?"

He wriggled out from under the dovecote, brushing off feathers and petrified pigeon droppings. Standing beside the dovecote was Febrys, lady-in-waiting to the queen and one of Kobold's demon spies. She was wearing a gown of blue-and-silver brocade. Febrys was fair of face and would have been beautiful had she not been so unnaturally pale: the pale hair that showed beneath the linen of her headdress was closer to white than gold, and her eyes were like clouds reflected in water. The twilight on the silver brocade made her look more eerie still, as though Kobold had fashioned her out of cold moonlight and dust. Which he probably had, Gideon thought.

"I thought I saw a fox slip under the pigeon coop," he said.

She looked him up and down like an owl eyeing a mouse. "A fox? But why not send your wyvern after it? Why begrime yourself when she could save you the trouble?" Her voice dripped with sweetness, but it reminded Gideon of the honey the palace cook used to cover the taste of meat that was rotten. He laughed and Febrys took a startled step backward. Laughter is a powerful charm against demons.

"Send a wyvern after a fox? That would raise an awful clamor, and something tells me our new queen wouldn't care to have her evening prayers disrupted in such a noisy fashion. In any case, there was no fox—I merely fancied I saw one. But you can see for yourself." He waved an arm toward the dovecote.

Febrys wrinkled her nose. "Of course I take you at your word, Gideon." She turned and walked away across the courtyard.

Gideon looked after her. He knew he had not deceived her. She would go straight to Kobold. There was no time to lose.

He started back to his rooms. The apparatus required to fetch a wyvern was elaborate and would take one wizard working alone most of the night to set up, but if he worked steadily, all would be ready by the hour just before dawn, when fetching spells are most effective.

He took a shortcut through the vegetable garden, and it was then that he saw the unearthly glimmer coming from the melon patch. Gideon felt his heart sink.

There was no mistaking it: the talon marks in the earth were Wycca's. And there was no mistaking the hazy ring of oily light, shimmering and humming faintly like a spinning top.

Gideon sat down among the melons with a groan. Wycca had gone through a bolt-hole, a kind of magical rabbit-hole through Time, into some other Where—and, what was much worse, some other When.

He had started to put his hand through the bolt-hole when he stopped himself. It was no use rushing after her unprepared. He went back to his chambers and spent an hour putting his crucibles and books away under lock and spell.

Wycca couldn't have chosen a more inconvenient moment to run away. He was supposed to judge the flight trials of the rising class of yearling dragons, settle a long-running dispute between humans and some trolls about mining rights, host a lavish banquet for visiting dignitaries from the dwarves, and preside over the new session of the Guild's high court. He hardly had any time at all to pursue his own studies in demon genealogy or perfect the new universal antidote. The last batch of the stuff had rendered the king's food taster weightless for a week. Gideon now understood why his predecessor had retired to the country to tend bees.

On a high shelf lay coiled a two-headed snake and beside it, under a bell jar, a cool blue flame that burned without air or fuel. These were Gideon's familiars, the Worm Ouroboros, as old as Time, and Ignus, an intelligent, biddable Fire.

Gideon paused in packing his satchel. He lifted the glass bell and held out an empty coin purse, making a soft clucking sound. Ignus flowed off the shelf and into the coin purse. Gideon snapped it shut and placed it in his pocket. Then he held out his arm for Ouroboros. The snake slid along his master's arm, arranging himself in coils underneath the sleeve of Gideon's tunic. There was a small hole in the seam where the sleeve was attached, and from this the snake could look out.

The wizard's last task was to compose a note to the king explaining his sudden absence. He spoiled two sheets of foolscap before he hit on a likely excuse: a summons to attend an emergency convocation of the Guild of Adepts in the Wizardly Arts. He supposed Kobold would see through it, but by then Gideon hoped he would be back, with Wycca in tow, in time to head off any attempt to overthrow him as Sorcerer Royal. Gideon deftly folded the note into the form of a dove, said a few words over it in Wizard's Latin, and watched the paper bird wing its way to the castle and into the king's chamber window.

He gave the cage of newts their freedom and left out a saucer of buttermilk, just in case Wycca hadn't gone through the bolt-hole after all.

"Lock up," he told the door, and, as the bolt obediently slid to, the wizard shouldered his satchel and made his way back to the melon patch.

2

Theodora, Known as Dodo

"WHY CAN'T I come with you?" Theodora Oglethorpe was sitting on the end of her father's bed, her legs folded pretzel fashion. She was sulking but finding it difficult to pout and at the same time admire her plastic vampire teeth in the mirror over the dresser.

Mr. Oglethorpe was packing Hawaiian shirts and hiking socks into a battered suitcase so patched with duct tape and plastered with old U.S. Customs stickers that you could barely see the scuffed leather underneath. A bright orange label with the word QUARANTINE had not quite been peeled off.

Most fathers would have said, "Dodo, it's too dangerous," or "You're too young," or "You'd just be in the way," but Mr. Oglethorpe just went over to the dresser and took out a stack of undershirts and boxer shorts. "Well, if you want to apply for a job with the expedition, tell me your qualifications. Do you speak Laotian, Ms. Oglethorpe?"

Theodora shook her head.

"Can you put up a tent in ten minutes flat? And if your tent blows away, construct a bamboo lean-to?"

Theodora took out her plastic fangs and made them tug and worry the bedspread, like a vampire terrier. "No."

"Can you whip up dinner for twenty from an eel and half a kilo of rice? You have to catch the eel yourself."

Theodora felt her face turn red. "No, but I could make plaster casts of footprints, like you taught me last summer, and help you check the mist nets, and pack up the specimens."

Andy Oglethorpe sat down on the bed beside his daughter. He was tall and long-limbed—he had played baseball in college—and he took the vampire teeth from her and set them on the dresser without having to get up.

Theodora looked from her dad to her own reflection in the mirror. Even without the vampire teeth, she didn't think she looked anything like him. When she was a toddler Theodora had her dad's sandy hair, but as she grew older her hair had gotten darker so that now all the Oglethorpe great-aunties said, my, didn't she have the Greenwood coloring, from her mother's side of the family. Which was the Oglethorpe great-aunties' way of saying she had her mom's dark hair and brown eyes without being pretty like her mom at all. Theodora frowned unconsciously and pushed her thick, wavy hair back from her face.

"You see, it's like this," he said, taking her hands in his. "There's hardly any money for this expedition, so everyone who comes has to be able to do at least nine or ten useful things: fix a broken Jeep axle, operate a short-wave radio, treat snakebite, play poker. You're incredibly handy, Dodo, but you really only know about eight useful things."

Theodora could feel a last protest welling up, a final, exasperated "It's not fair," but she made herself swallow the words. You were allowed to sulk in the Oglethorpe household, and even to raise your voice, but under no circumstances were you allowed to whine.

"Madeleine *Silverfern* gets to go with *her* dad," she muttered.

As soon as the words were out of her mouth, Mr. Oglethorpe's face got a stubborn, shut-down look to it. He dropped her hands and stood up. "Well, we both know who her dad is, don't we? Go bother Mikko and let me finish packing."

Theodora walked slowly down the hall to the kitchen, where Mikko was making dinner.

Mikko had arrived on their doorstep four years ago, when Theodora was seven, in answer to an ad Mr. Oglethorpe had placed in the paper for a nanny. She "lived in," which meant she shared a room off the kitchen with her blue-eyed cat, Frankie. Mikko had long, straight blond hair and dark, almond-shaped eyes. Her ancestry was not Japanese; her real name, which Theodora knew because she had once found her driver's license in the clothes dryer, was Michelle Kolodney, but she had asked them to call her Mikko.

It was all very mysterious, and if you tried to get behind the mystery, Mikko would either change the subject or offer some version of her past that couldn't possibly be true. She hadn't *really* dropped out of high school to sail on a freighter to Tahiti—had she? And Theodora was almost certain Mikko was fibbing when she told the story about how her parents first met—that her mom was a circus acrobat who'd fallen from the trapeze, and her dad was the doctor who was bending over her when she woke up from her coma—but then the Oglethorpes' housekeeper *could* do a mean back flip.

Once her friend Val had asked Theodora if she thought her dad and Mikko might fall in love and get married and Theodora had thought about it for a long minute and said no, mostly because she couldn't picture Mikko drinking coffee in an ancient green chenille bathrobe instead of drinking tea in a kimono with origami cranes all over it.

Mikko was the kind of person who could do at least a hundred useful things. If she hadn't been a nanny, Theodora often thought, she would have made a good spy. Right now she was standing at the counter of their sunny kitchen making sushi. She was wearing her work uniform of loose black pajamas and white slip-on Keds, and a single bangle bracelet of milky green jade that chimed now and then against the counter or the sink faucet. Theodora watched her roll up slivers of crabmeat and avocado with rice in glossy green sheets of seaweed and then cut the roll into pieces that she placed on a wooden serving block.

Making sushi was one of the useful things Mikko could do. She could also hear through walls. She said, without turning around, "That probably wasn't the best strategy, Dodo. Bringing up the Silverfish."

Theodora picked up one of the shiny sheets of dried seaweed and held it up to the light. "Don't rub it in."

The Silverfish was Madeleine Silverfern's father, Malcolm Silverfern, head of the zoology department at the university and—even more important to the Oglethorpe household—head of the tenure committee. According to Mikko, the Silverfish was the reason that Theodora's father wasn't a full professor yet. What they all knew, and what no one talked about, was that if he wasn't made professor soon, Mr. Oglethorpe would have to find a job at another university, probably in some other state.

Theodora rolled the sheet of seaweed into a megaphone and spoke into the narrow end, pointing the open end of the cone at Mikko. "What if Dad finds some new kind of animal in Laos? Something no one else knew existed."

Mikko took the seaweed sheet away from her and began to make another sushi roll. "He could name it after you," said Mikko. *"Something-or-other theodoraensis."*

"But what if he found something big—not just some new kind of beetle. It would be a big deal. The Silverfish would have to make him a professor."

"Maybe." Mikko opened a jar and lifted out a limp, pink slice of pickled ginger with her chopsticks, and deftly twirled the slice into a small rose.

"It could happen," Theodora said. "They didn't think there were any mammals unknown to science, and then they found that new kind of deer in Vietnam and that monkey in South America."

"Well, your father might discover something. But it might or might not make a difference, Dodo."

"We can only hope," said Mr. Oglethorpe from the doorway. "Mikko, you really shouldn't go to so much trouble. We'd be just as happy with fish sticks."

Mikko tilted her head to one side, considering the

wooden block with its carefully composed arrangement of sushi. Her expression was carefully composed too. It was usually hard to guess what Mikko was thinking.

"It relaxes me," she said. "Like making origami, only you can eat it."

After dinner Theodora and her father walked into Inman Square for ice cream at Coneheads. Carrie, the owner, seemed surprised to see them, but she just made chitchat as she dished up their cones. The three Oglethorpes had been regular customers when Theodora's mother was alive, but after she died Theodora and her father had stayed away for a long time.

The wooden seats of their old corner booth were still shiny from countless bottoms scooting in and out. They ate their ice cream slowly, without speaking, because it felt so familiar and so strange to be there, just the two of them. Theodora smiled a tiny smile and her dad smiled back.

Later that evening, when he came in to kiss her good night, Mr. Oglethorpe had to clear a spot on the edge of the bed before he could sit down. He gathered up a slithery pile of videodiscs, GameBot cartridges, and holographic trading cards and transferred them carefully to the surface of her desk. Something fluttered to the floor.

"What's this?" he asked, holding up a small printed square of plastic. The light from the bedside lamp shone through it.

"It's a wyvernkeeper's Guild Tattoo," said Theodora. "It washes off eventually."

Mr. Oglethorpe shook his head. "Dodo, I thought you weren't going to spend any more of your allowance on this dragon junk."

"*Wyvern* junk." Theodora took the tattoo and placed it carefully in the ever-expanding shrine of wyvernalia under the window. "And, anyway, I didn't spend my allowance on it. It came free in the cereal."

Mr. Oglethorpe rolled his eyes. "Sometimes I wish I'd never taken you to see that movie. I hope you'll turn the video off long enough to notice that it's summer vacation."

To Theodora's delight, he said this under the outspread wings of the papier-mâché wyvern she had made in art class. The wyvern had used up two whole Sunday editions of the *Boston Globe,* and it had a wingspan of almost six feet. Its open beak was only inches from the top of Mr. Oglethorpe's head.

"I don't want to come back to find you've turned into one of those blind salamanders that lives in caves. You'd have to give up cereal with wyvern marshmallows and start eating flies."

Theodora slid down under the sheets. "If you take

me to Laos with you, I'll leave all my wyvern stuff behind. Even my trading cards."

Mr. Oglethorpe kissed her good night and stood in the doorway with his hand on the light switch. "You're lucky I didn't take Aunt Mariah up on her offer to send you to French camp. Now go to sleep."

The next morning they all piled into the car with all the luggage for the drive to the airport. Mr. Oglethorpe was flying to New York to join up with some other scientists for the long flight to Laos. At the security gate Mikko discreetly hung back while Theodora and her father said good-bye.

"Squeeze you," said Mr. Oglethorpe, hugging his daughter and lifting her off the ground.

"Squeeze you back," said Theodora as he set her back down.

Then Mr. Oglethorpe waved at Mikko and said, "See you in August," and disappeared through the metal detector.

On the ride home Theodora was very quiet except for an occasional deep sigh. It was shaping up to be a truly lousy summer. Her two best friends—and who was she kidding, they were her *only* friends—were going to be away until the week before school started. Milo was spending ten weeks with his mother and stepfather in

Calgary, Alberta, and Valerie was being held prisoner at an orchestra camp in the Adirondacks.

As another deep sigh echoed from the backseat, Mikko glanced into the rearview mirror. Theodora had slid so far down in her seat that the top of her head was barely visible.

"I brought some bread," Mikko said, cutting off the next sigh. "Shall we go feed the ducks?"

They drove to Mount Auburn, the big Victorian cemetery not far from Harvard Square. Mikko parked the car, and they walked up the path to their favorite duck pond, passing graves marked with marble urns, lambs, obelisks, rose-covered crosses, melancholy angels, and even tiny Greek temples. For a cemetery, Mount Auburn really wasn't very spooky, with the sunlight filtering through the branches of the huge, old chestnuts and oaks and robins bounding along on the brilliant green carpets of grass between the graves.

Mikko and Theodora took off their shoes and dabbled their toes in the duckweed, tearing off chunks of bread and tossing them to the resident mallards. Mikko was an accomplished cat-napper, and in a few moments she was lying back on the grassy bank, her sunglasses slightly askew, snoring. Theodora had soon forgotten all about her father going off to the Laotian jungle to discover exciting new creatures without her. She was imagining instead that she was an apprentice wyvernkeeper, second class, dangling her feet off a drawbridge into a moat, tossing bread to the resident dragon.

Thus occupied, neither Mikko nor Theodora noticed a growing disturbance not far from them. Crows had been gathering by the dozen in a nearby oak, bobbing and cawing, until they filled its branches. They were used to mobbing birds of prey and driving off any red-tailed hawks that tried to set up housekeeping in the cemetery. But this time, as they attempted to flush the intruder hiding deep among the innermost branches, there was a warning sound, something between a snake's hiss and a lion's roar, and a plume of flame shot out from the greenery like water from a fire hose. One crow fell to the ground, startled and singed but otherwise unhurt, and the rest fled squawking.

Hidden in the oak, Wycca pondered her plight. This spot had looked quite promising—water, plenty of perches, and groundskeepers and bird-watchers to tease—but there wasn't enough privacy. As soon as it was dark she would have to move on, and find a more suitable place for hatching magic.

3

The Wizard of Harvard Square

THE TRIP THROUGH the bolt-hole lasted less than the blink of an eye. One moment Gideon was in the melon patch behind the castle, and the next he was being jostled this way and that on the smoky, strobe-lit dance floor of the Club Golgotha in Central Square, Cambridge, Massachusetts. To a wizard from the thirteenth century, there was little to distinguish the club's dark, cavernous interior and its ghoulish inhabitants from the court of a demon king.

Gideon was hemmed in by the sea of thrashing bodies, unable to move. Despite the appearance of those around him—their faces pierced and painted, their wild hair silver and green and blue—he did not think they were demons. For one thing, they did not have the spoiled-cabbage-and-brimstone smell peculiar to demons.

Whether they were possessed or just writhing in pain from the banshee wails that filled the air, Gideon did not linger to find out. Patting his sleeve to make sure Ouroboros was still safely wrapped around his arm, the wizard held tight to his knapsack and struck out through the crowd. Halfway to the door he was startled to feel someone picking his pocket. He yelped in protest, but his cry was drowned out by the din, and the thief had already vanished into the crush.

Gideon realized that, in his haste to go after Wycca, he had failed to take any traveling wizard's first precaution against thieves, and say a durable, waterproofing binding spell over the contents of his pockets. Chiding himself for his carelessness, he whistled a high-pitched *Fwwwft,* and his coin purse leaped back into his hand. He gathered his cloak more tightly about him and with a final push gained the door and the rain-slick street.

"Ouroboros," said Gideon, glancing at the streetlights that stretched high overhead. "What are these strange torches?"

Ouroboros emerged from the sleeve of Gideon's tunic and coiled himself loosely around the wizard's neck. The snake consulted his vast memory, which functioned as efficiently forward into the future as it did back into the past.

"A kind of tamed lightning they call electricity," he said. "It was first harnessed about a century ago, for use in lamps, but they have since trained it to carry voices along wires and paint moving tapestries on glass."

Gideon furrowed his brow. "Is it biddable, like Ignus?"

"Yes, but I fear it is neither agile nor intelligent. We should approach it with caution."

"I see."

To this newly acquired concept, *electricity,* Gideon added in rapid succession *car, bus, escalator,* and *subway.* Getting through the subway turnstile without a token was a matter of a simple charm, and to the wizard's relief, his clothes—a cloak, tunic, and hose, all in black wool—did not seem to attract too much attention. In fact, he had noticed several people in similar garb back in the club. One young woman in the subway car did seem to be fascinated by his scarlet shoes with their long, turned-up toes.

They got off at Harvard Square, because the map in the Central Square station had indicated there was a university there. Where there was a university, there would be books, and very likely the chief wizard of this realm. Gideon would need his permission—and possibly even his protection—in order to accomplish his errand in this strange future.

The moving stairs deposited Gideon a few yards from an open-air stall selling all the news of the day, written on large thin sheets in handwriting so even and small, it seemed that all the angels in heaven must have been employed to copy it out. The stall itself was shuttered, but a man was unloading neatly tied bundles. Gideon peered at the nearest.

"The Boston Globe," he read aloud, "June 17, 2002." He was suddenly so dizzy that he had to sit down where he was, on the bricks of the large square. The wizard's head throbbed, and he felt quite sick to his stomach.

He heard the voice of Ouroboros in his ear. "You're time-sick," the snake hissed, "and very likely future-sick, too. A trip through the bolt-hole will do that to you."

Gideon clutched his pounding head. He ought to have read up on future-sickness before he'd stepped through the bolt-hole; his memory of the symptoms was fuzzy, but he seemed to recall a diminishment of wizardly powers was one of them. The wizard groaned. All he needed was to be even *more* vulnerable while he searched for his runaway wyvern. All around him the tamed lightning electricity flashed in all its garish forms: in lighted signs, in commands to walk and to stop, in the strange glowing eyes of the mechanical carts, called *cars,* that sped murderously around the streets. The wizard cowered beside the bundle of newspapers, unable to move.

Footsteps approached across the expanse of brick, and Gideon found himself staring at the toes of a highly polished pair of shoes. Slowly, he raised his eyes.

He saw a short, balding man, dressed all in brown and carrying a rectangular leather case by a handle. Across his arm was hung the curved end of a long, pointed black object that seemed to be fashioned of pleated black silk. Gideon found himself being studied with great interest by a pair of pale blue eyes, greatly magnified behind the glass of a very thick pair of spectacles (though Gideon would only learn that they were called *spectacles* some time later).

This portly apparition removed its hat and bowed deeply. "May I introduce myself? Iain Merlin O'Shea, professor emeritus of medieval history and folklore at Harvard University, at your service! Bolt-holes are a bit of a hobby with me," he explained. "I was just about to get on the subway to see who or what had come through to this When from some other one. But not only do I discover you sitting practically on my own doorstep, I find you are a brother in the Guild, too! The last time I detected someone coming through that bolt-hole—not a system of my own invention, just elementary bells-and-spells, though I have made one or *two* refinements—it turned out to be an overripe melon. It appeared on a bar stool and one of the other patrons was gallantly trying to converse with it."

Then Gideon saw it, pinned to the lapel of the brown tweed suit that Professor O'Shea wore on even the warmest summer evenings: a small jeweled emblem, an owl grasping a crystal ball—the unmistakable mark of the Guild of Adepts in the Wizardly Arts. By some good fortune, he had chanced upon the Wizard of Harvard Square.

"You look as though you could do with a cup of tea," said Merlin as he helped pull Gideon to his feet.

"Tea?" said Gideon, looking blankly at his rescuer.

"Forgive me," said Professor O'Shea, heading away down the sidewalk at a rapid clip. "You are from, when, 1279 or so? England and the rest of Europe won't learn about tea until 1644 or then-abouts. I think you will find it a uniquely revivifying potion." He raised his umbrella in the air with a flourish and cried, "Taxi!"

Gideon leaped back just as one of the mechanical carts lurched to a stop at the curb. The professor lifted a silver handle on one side of the cart and the door swung open.

"Do get in," Merlin said when Gideon hesitated. "My rooms are just a short walk from here, but in your condition I don't think you should attempt it."

The journey through the streets of Cambridge was

far more terrifying than the instantaneous trip through the bolt-hole, and Gideon emerged from the taxi at 23½ Agassiz Street amazed to find himself in one piece. On the ride he had learned that this kingdom—which was not a kingdom—was called America and that the driver of the cab was from a distant land called Hay-Tee.

Merlin led the way into a tall brick building and motioned for Gideon to precede him into a small room. It was barely large enough to hold them both and was empty of any furnishings. Gideon was thinking this was all very strange when Merlin pressed a button in the wall. Suddenly, the doors closed of their own accord, and the whole room began to rise.

Ouroboros emerged from Gideon's collar. "A moving room, like the moving stairs," he explained. "It's called an elevator."

"I see you have your own time interpreter," said Merlin. "Very handy."

They emerged into a long corridor lined with doors. Merlin took a key from his pocket and opened one of the doors farthest away from the elevator.

Like a desert wanderer stumbling upon an oasis, Gideon stepped across the threshold into a room full of comfortingly familiar things. His eyes drank in the fine thirteenth-century French and English oak furniture, the elegant tapestries, and the shelves sagging beneath the weight of vast numbers of leather-bound books. A haven of his own time, he thought. But then he noticed that the flickering torchlight cast on the walls was actually electric.

"I have made a few concessions to the twenty-first century," Merlin confessed. "Now have a seat and tell me what brings you across an ocean and seven centuries into the future."

First Gideon made his companions comfortable. Ignus was released from the coin purse to stretch and flicker beneath an upturned brandy snifter on the fireplace mantel, while Ouroboros slithered from Gideon's neck onto a new perch on the coatrack. Then Gideon accepted a cup of tea, sat back upon the cushioned bench, and told his tale to the Wizard of Harvard Square.

Merlin thoughtfully drummed the fingertips of one hand against the fingertips of the other. "I really ought to report your arrival to the Northeastern Central Subbranch officer, you know."

Gideon shook his head. "I fear I am even now being followed. Can you report my presence after I've left?"

"I will do you one even better," said Merlin. "I simply will report you as a Class Seven Time-place Aberration Event, which in plain parlance means the bolthole under surveillance hiccupped without dispensing anything or anyone in this Where and When. It will keep your mischief from catching up with you, if we're lucky, and it will save me no end of paperwork."

"Won't the Guild mind if they find out?" Gideon asked.

"I am afraid the Guild is sadly diminished in stature from the organization you knew," said Merlin. "The sorts of people elected to the highest posts are the kinds of wizards you'd never want to have as your lab partner in introductory vanishing-and-reappearing. Forming commissions to argue about the meaning of a single word in a spell no one uses anymore, when there's a desperate need to recruit and train wizards in more practical aspects of sorcery. Most good wizards—the ones who really care about their craft—end up going freelance after a while."

"Why do you stay, then?" asked Gideon.

"Some of us are trying—trying, mind you—to reform the Guild from within, reestablish specialties in some of the forgotten crafts, such as shape-shifting. Once wizards are all freelancers and there are no longer Convocations, we have little chance of really keeping an eye on the bolt-holes, let alone all the other Wild Magic. Before when something slipped through that wasn't meant to mix with mortals, it could be contained for a while without doing much harm. But today news can spread around the globe, by mortal means, in the blink of an eye. There aren't enough of us, so part of G.A.W.A.'s mission, as we see it, is to identify the new generation of wizards.

"But enough about G.A.W.A.'s woes—we need to find that runaway wyvern of yours."

Gideon nodded. "It should be a simple matter of setting up the apparatus and performing a Fetching. Though I will need to borrow a few items. My fetching kit is lacking a basilisk feather and fresh eye of newt."

Merlin O'Shea shook his head mournfully. "Oh, dear," he said, "I'm afraid it will be next to impossible to find either one Here and Now."

"Why impossible?"

"There are no more basilisks—they were hunted to extinction back in the 1600s. As for newts—well, they're hanging on, but they're on the endangered species list. You can't kill one, not without a lot of bothersome permits saying you need to sacrifice it for the good of science. But don't look so crestfallen. Old Merlin will find a way. After all, one can't have one's wyvern wandering loose in such a future as this."

No, thought Gideon, not when an enemy like Kobold could get wind of it, even across an ocean and seven centuries.

It was a beautiful, cool summer night. The thin clouds had all scudded away to reveal a deep blue curtain hung with brilliant stars. Wycca sniffed the salt air, happily exhausted from the effort of enlarging and relining her nest. Granted, it had been previously occupied, but it was well worth all the trouble to remodel. Her chosen nesting spot was high above the city, far from prying eyes, in a tower that offered a spectacular view of the harbor.

Granted, too, the pair of peregrine falcons she had kicked out had given her some grief, claiming squatters' rights to the spot, but a single fiery "Ahem" had served to singe their feathers and change their minds. They had departed, leaving Wycca a plentiful supply of fine peregrine down with which to line her nest—and not a moment too soon.

Wycca shifted on the nest, trying to make herself comfortable. This was tricky, for she was perched on an object a little larger than a good-sized cantaloupe and slightly pointed at one end, the palest silver-green hue speckled with lavender: the most beautiful, most precious egg in the world.

The wyvern closed her eyes, stretched her jaws in a yawn, and began to make the low rumbling sound that is a dragon's equivalent of purring.

4

The Usefulness of Wyverns

IT SHOULD HAVE been her father who couldn't sleep. But while Andy Oglethorpe slept soundly, stretched across three seats on a jumbo jet thousands of feet above the dark ocean, it was Theodora who lay awake. At midnight, long after she should have been asleep, she sat cross-legged on her bed with her *Wizards & Wyverns* cards spread out on the quilt like a magical game of solitaire. The deck had twenty-eight cards—skimpy compared to a regular deck of fifty-two, until you remembered that each card represented a twenty-six ounce box of *Wizards & Wyverns* cereal with marshmallows.

Along the foot of the bed Theodora had laid out in a row the seven cards that made up the Wyvern suit: Red, Green, Purple, Silver, Gold, Black, and White. The other three suits ran down below each Wyvern card, representing the traits of each dragon: its Power, its Frailty, and the magical Wand needed to tame it (you needed a silver wand for the Silver Wyvern, an emerald wand for the Green Wyvern, and so on). You needed all three trait cards for each suit before you could tame that wyvern.

Once she had tamed all seven, Theodora would be able to join the Wyvernkeeper's Circle, the club that met in the back room of Traveler's Tales, the comic and fantasy game store upstairs from a dry cleaner's in Davis Square. Since two of the cards were almost impossible to get, it was hard to get into the Circle. She knew it would probably be a terrible letdown if she ever did get inside. There were a couple of kids at school who wore Wyvernkeeper's Circle patches on their backpacks, and their faces had a pasty, greenish look, as though they didn't get outside enough. How much fun could it be, sitting around talking to *them*? But Theodora just couldn't help it: She wanted to know she could join if she wanted to.

She was missing only the Power card for the Black Wyvern. It was her favorite card of the Wyvern suit, the dragon shown curled up high on the ramparts of a castle under a crescent moon. The Wand card for the Black Wyvern was onyx and its Frailty was sunlight, so it could be ridden only by moonlight. A few weeks earlier Theodora had tried making her own Power card for it, first by scanning the Power card for the Silver Wyvern and trying to doctor it using the painting software on her dad's computer, and then the old-fashioned way, with Bristol board and expensive watercolors borrowed from Mikko. She hadn't been happy with the results, and when she'd stormed off to her room in frustration, her father had given her a lecture (which she had heard before) about how fast fun made you lose touch with your imagination the way fast food wrecked your taste buds.

"But I didn't want it to look just like the other cards," she had said to Mikko. "I wanted it to look *better.*"

This was after her attempts had been retrieved from the trash and they were standing at the kitchen sink, cleaning Mikko's good sable paintbrushes.

"What did you want it to look like?" Mikko had asked.

Theodora had only shrugged, suddenly too shy to say that she had wanted it to look like one of the small, jeweled paintings in the medieval manuscript gallery at the Museum of Fine Arts.

She was stifling a yawn and starting to gather up the cards when the door opened a crack and Mikko looked in. Mikko's nightclothes were a lot like her work uniform, except the pajamas she actually slept in were white. She had traded her Keds for a pair of red brocade dragon slippers, and in her arms she held a large white cat.

"You're up late," she observed, coming in and looking down at the cards spread out on the bed. "Couldn't you sleep?"

Theodora shook her head.

Mikko sat on the edge of the bed, and the cat climbed out of her arms onto the quilt, stepping carefully around the cards. Soon he was treading a sleeping spot on the quilt, his large blue eyes fixed on Theodora.

"Well, Frankie seems ready to bunk down here for the night. Okay with you?"

Theodora nodded her head vigorously. Frankie had the run of the apartment but seldom left his favorite spot in the chair by Mikko's bedroom window.

Theodora gathered up the cards and returned them to their drawstring bag of purple velvet. Mikko returned the bag to the wyvern shrine under the window, then paused with her hand on the door.

"Good night, Dodo."

Standing silhouetted in the light from the hall, Mikko looked a little like Theodora's mother. Even a little was way too much. Theodora quickly rolled over to face the wall and mumbled "Good night" into the covers.

—~—

As it happened, Gideon had his own deck of wyvern cards, but they were quite unlike Theodora's. Like Theodora's deck, these were a little larger than baseball cards, but instead of cardboard, his were made out of thin pieces of ivory painted in jewel-like colors. The deck had thirty-three cards. In addition to the four regular suits—Earth, Air, Fire, and Water, each with its own king, queen, knight, page, jester, and wizard—there were seven Dragon trumps: the griffin, basilisk, wyvern, firedrake, cockatrice, chimera, and gorgon. The deck also had two wild cards, but instead of jokers, they were demons, one red and one black.

Gideon would not have known what to make of Theodora's deck, with its Powers and Frailties and Wands that had little to do with his experience of dragons. Dragons certainly had their weaknesses: for instance, basilisks are scared of cats and manticores won't fly. But a quality Theodora would call a Power, Gideon was used to thinking of as a Talent. Griffins could be used to sniff out veins of gold in the earth, much the way pigs snuffle for truffles, and chimeras have a particularly musical purr—good for singing cranky babies to sleep.

But of all the dragons, wyverns were by far the most useful, and the most desirable for the purposes of wizardry. A good wyvern was like a cross between the swiftest falcon and the most tireless hunting dog, but instead of a quarry of rabbits, wyverns were trained to seek out and seize all manner of the smaller demons and to sniff out and corner unfettered spells. They were invaluable to a wizard in his daily work. Once trained, a wyvern answered only to the wizard who had collared it—except through a procedure, banned since the Dublin Convocation of 1420, called a Turning, in which a wyvern who had strayed beyond the range of its master's magic was captured and turned against him. From that point onward, the wyvern's former master would become its quarry and it would pursue him at all costs. If the dragon caught him, it was usually the end of them both.

Thoughts like these were keeping Gideon from getting much sleep. He and Merlin had talked past midnight, until Merlin had bade him good night and retreated to his room with his ritual cocoa and crossword. Now, in the gray hours of early morning, Gideon woke from a troubled dream. As it faded he sent a spell after it, to tether it to his memory, but whether the dream was charmed itself or his spellcasting suffered from the trip through the bolt-hole, it nearly slipped from his mind's grasp.

His spell was only able to retrieve a small snippet. Kobold, a poxy, raw-boned apprentice of sixteen, was dressed as a fool, putting on a show with wooden puppets carved in the form of demons. Behind him more puppets—a wizard, a wyvern, a maiden—swung by their strings from hooks, waiting a turn in the show. Who was the puppet show for? The audience, whether one spectator or many, was in shadow.

Gideon sat up and rubbed his temples, listening to the sounds of cars passing outside and the electric hum of the refrigerator. At last he threw off the blankets and called for his Fire. Ignus flowed down from the mantelpiece and collected at Gideon's elbow in a cool blue puddle of flame.

"Light," commanded Gideon, and Ignus obediently stretched himself into a torch of cool light. Being magical, the illumination Ignus gave off was not the best light by which to work. Merlin's lamps gave off a much warmer, natural light, but Gideon did not yet trust the electricity that ran them.

"Brighter and less blue," he said, and as if to tease him, Ignus dimmed and glowed a deep cobalt before forming a ball of silver fire, like strong moonlight. He rose to hover just at the wizard's shoulder.

"Stay." Gideon laid out the cards in a T formation, first laying down one card and dealing three cards to the left of it and three to the right of it, for a row of seven, and then dealing another six straight down from the center card, for a total of thirteen. What he saw in the cards did not reassure him, and he pushed them away from him in a jumble before falling asleep.

Gideon usually kept the deck carefully wrapped in a

piece of blue velvet and tied with a silver cord, but in his haste to get to the bolt-hole, he had seized the deck and thrust it into his pocket without bothering to tie it securely. What he failed to see as he dealt the cards was that one of them was missing. In his own When and Where he would have noticed the difference in the cards immediately—they would have felt different the moment he picked them up. But the wizard attributed the unpleasant queasy feeling that came over him to future-sickness. And when the cards themselves tried to alert their master to the card missing from the deck by conspiring to fly off the table in a sudden phantom gust, Gideon picked them up, scolding them, but failed to notice one thing.

The wyvern trump was not among them.

Theodora slept late the next day, and it was only the smell of breakfast that roused her from bed. She stumbled into the kitchen, arms stretched out in front of her.

"Me smell flesh," she droned in her best zombie tone.

"You smell French toast," said Mikko, sliding it onto a plate and setting it in front of her.

The French toast was stuffed with sweetened cream cheese and blueberries. As Theodora dug in, Mikko set a large glass of grapefruit juice at her place.

"When you're done, hurry and get dressed."

"Suit, shorts, sandals?" said Theodora. This was the family shorthand for a swim at Walden Pond.

"Clothes without holes will do," said Mikko.

Mikko herself had changed into a green linen sundress and espadrilles printed all over with clusters of cherries. She had pulled her hair back into a ponytail tied with a green chiffon scarf.

"You've never worn that outfit before," Theodora said. Her own jeans and T-shirt suddenly seemed hopelessly boring.

Mikko shrugged. "Well, you mostly see me in my work clothes. When I'm not on the job I like to dress up a little."

"You're on the job now," Theodora pointed out.

"Well, think of it as my uniform for field trips."

"Are we going on a field trip?" Theodora asked, buckling up.

Mikko fished in her purse and took out a pair of cat's-eye sunglasses. She put them on and then turned the key in the ignition. "You'll see."

It was a beautiful day, with big, starchy clouds scooting briskly through the sky, like ships on the ocean. Theodora sat in the backseat, looking out the window and stealing a glance at Mikko from time to time. Seeing her out of her work clothes made Theodora suddenly think of her as someone she didn't know after all. Like seeing a teacher at the supermarket or at the movies. Of course Theodora knew Mikko had a past—she had an ex-fiancé and one and a half Ph.D.s—but Theodora suddenly wondered about Mikko's everyday, ordinary past.

What were her mom and dad like? Were there other Kolodneys, brothers and sisters? If Mikko went out on dates on her night off, she never talked about it. Theodora suddenly realized she didn't even know if Mikko had gotten Frankie as a kitten or adopted him from a shelter. And Theodora also realized how hard Mikko worked to keep her life private, without you ever noticing that she was doing it.

They drove north along the coast to Salem, where they spent a few hours in the Peabody Essex Museum, looking at an exhibit of miniatures from India, paintings no bigger than a playing card, bursting with life and color: vivid silk saris, strolling peacocks, fountains, tiled courtyards, blue-skinned gods, and gold-striped tigers. Afterward they bought some postcards from the gift shop and strolled through the heart of town, past souvenir shops selling Salem witch T-shirts and Frightening Fudge.

At last they came to a neighborhood of narrow brick houses shaded by old oak trees. Mikko stopped at a house with pink and white geraniums in the window boxes and a brass dolphin on its green door. Mikko picked up the heavy knocker and rapped out two loud knocks.

The sound was met on the other side of the door by a noisy scrabble of paws on tile, frantic, high-pitched barking, and a scolding voice as the bolt was turned. The door opened to reveal a tiny Indian woman with glossy black hair, wearing a sari of fuchsia-and-green silk bordered in silver and a pair of high-tech running shoes. Hiding in her skirts were two little black and white dogs with sharp little muzzles and enormous ears. They darted out to leap at the intruders, quivering with so much indignation that Theodora laughed aloud.

"Kip, Rudy, get down!" said the woman. "Mikko, how lovely to see you." Mikko put her palms together in a traditional Indian gesture of greeting and bowed over them. Then she made introductions.

"Dr. Naga, this is Theodora Oglethorpe. Dodo, this is Dr. Naga," said Mikko. "She was one of my teachers at art school."

"Hello," said Theodora shyly.

"Pleased to meet you, my dear," said Dr. Naga. "But then, Mikko has told me so much about you, I feel as though I already know you. Won't you come in?"

She led them through a series of small rooms crammed with books and paintings and CDs and musical instruments to a sun-dappled courtyard where a wicker table and chairs were set among planters of bougainvillea and jasmine.

Mikko and Dr. Naga had quite a bit of catching up to do, and while they sat and traded news about people Theodora didn't know, she wrestled with Kip and Rudy, who had stopped seeing her as an alien intruder and were doing their best to lick her to death.

"But I am forgetting my manners," said Dr. Naga. "On a warm day you will be wanting a cooling drink."

She went inside, followed by the two dogs, and reappeared with a pitcher of fizzy limeade. It wasn't ice cold, and it was very slightly salty, but by the end of her second glass, Theodora liked it.

"Now, Theodora, tell me, did you like the paintings at the Peabody Essex?" Dr. Naga asked.

Theodora nodded vigorously. "Yes—especially the one of the girls playing tricks on the demons."

"Ah, yes, yes," said Dr. Naga, smiling. "Outwitting demons is a very useful skill for a young girl." The way her eyes sparkled as she said this, you might have thought Dr. Naga had outwitted a few demons herself. "Mikko said you might like to see the studio. Will you follow me?"

The studio was at the top of the house, in an octagonal turret with windows on all sides. The room held only a drawing table, a rolling taboret of artist's supplies, and a boom box set on the floor. In a small well on the drawing table, meant to hold a bottle of ink, was a small porcelain cup half full of tea. On the drawing table, held down with pins in the four corners, was a miniature in progress showing the god Krishna wrestling with a water dragon.

Theodora couldn't say anything at first. You needed a magnifying glass to see all the detail: Krishna himself was only the size of a dime, and the individual scales on the water dragon were the size of the smallest beads at the bead store in Harvard Square.

"It's wonderful. You did this?"

Dr. Naga nodded. "It took me many years of training. I left art school to learn how to paint in the old style. At that time it was quite unfashionable. They all thought I was mad. Would you like to watch me work?"

Theodora drew up a stool and watched as Dr. Naga filled in the scales on the dragon's tail, using a swiveling lighted magnifying glass and working with the smallest paintbrushes Theodora had ever seen. Then she held out a brush to Theodora.

"Would you like to try it?"

"Oh, no, I couldn't," said Theodora. "My hand always shakes, and it never comes out right."

But Dr. Naga gently insisted, and soon Theodora was sitting at the drawing table and Dr. Naga was showing her how much paint to take up on the brush and how to steady her painting hand with her free hand.

Theodora very carefully added three scales to the water dragon. They weren't exactly like the other scales, but they weren't terrible, either.

"Talent is really the least of it," Dr. Naga said. "It's really more training and patience and having the best tools. And you have to allow yourself to be very, very bad at it, at the beginning. All the discipline in the universe will be of no use to you if you cannot allow yourself to make mistakes." She looked up at Mikko and laughed. "Am I sounding too much like Yoda? Well, I think I have dispensed enough wisdom for one day!"

5

The Forgotten Art of Fetching

BACK AT THE Agassiz Arms, Merlin and Gideon were having a late breakfast.

"You must realize," said Merlin, spreading a thick layer of marmalade on a piece of toast, "that fetching is a neglected art in the twenty-first century."

They were sitting in the sleek tiled kitchen of the elder wizard's apartment. Here there was no trace of the thirteenth century—no soot-blackened walls or open hearth with a leg of mutton turning on a spit. It was all gleaming chrome, with a row of strange mechanical devices devoted to the alchemy of turning the raw into the cooked without significant human effort.

Gideon's only reply was a distracted "Uh-hum." He was staring at the toaster, waiting for his third slice of toast to spring up at the chime of an invisible bell. Merlin himself usually breakfasted on cornflakes and a banana and black coffee, but as Indian maize and the coffee bean were two more New World plants unknown to thirteenth-century Europe, he had offered his guest toast with strawberry jam and tea—kinder to a medieval stomach recuperating from a bad case of future-sickness.

"Part of the problem, of course, is the lack of wyverns and other dragons to fetch. When witch-hunting was in its heyday, the Guild of Adepts frowned on fetching—it was too easily confused with the summoning of demons and other so-called black sorcery—and by the time they smiled on it again, all the big dragons were gone. Most people couldn't be bothered to stage a full-scale Fetching for such runty game as basilisks."

Ouroboros and Ignus were on the countertop, where the two-headed snake was absorbed in his own breakfast (a soft-scrambled egg with a few drops of chili sauce and a saucer of tea with plenty of milk). Ignus never ate anything—being magical, he burned without consuming any fuel—and while the snake was eating he was exploring the stove. At first he mistook the blue flame that leaped up so obediently for an intelligent fire, like himself, and was a little shocked that it should be put to such drudgery as boiling water. But once Merlin had explained that it was a dumb fire, stored in a special tank as gas, the intelligent flame was fascinated and kept dancing around the burners, trying to draw the stupid fire out.

"And, of course," Merlin continued, "the market for fetching apparatuses all but dried up, and the best artisans stopped making the equipment altogether."

When Gideon had finished his fourth piece of toast, Merlin placed their mugs and jam-sticky plates into a chest to be magically washed. He had to open the door of the dishwasher several times to show Gideon how it worked.

They went into the tapestry-lined study, where Merlin took down from a shelf a small book bound in sheepskin. Gideon recognized it as the Guild's official guide to fetching, *Fetching, Summoning, and Sundry Spells of Binding,* otherwise known as *F.S.S.S.B.*

"This is, of course, *F.S.S.S.B. Four,* the Edinburgh revision of 1749," said Merlin, "but I am sure you would recognize most of it. One Convocation changes something, and then the next one just changes it back." He sat at the broad oak slab supported by carved griffins that served as his desk and workbench and leafed carefully through the fragile pages.

"Hmm . . . hmm . . . yes, it's as I thought." He shut the book. "If we can come up with most of the equipment, and if we're willing to perform the full-length Fetching, without any of the abbreviations of the Toledo Convocation of 1520, we can make a few substitutions for the missing eye of newt and basilisk feather. Now, what equipment did you bring with you?"

Gideon retrieved his satchel from the chair by the fire and spread its contents out upon the carpet.

He had not set off for the future unprepared. There was a purse full of the sort of slightly lopsided old coins you sometimes see in museums, only these were shiny and new; a tin box containing tinder and flint for lighting a fire; a medieval first-aid kit of linen bandages and herbal ointments; a strange contraption, part bridle and part muzzle, fashioned of leather and golden chain mail; a coil of light strong silver cable; and last but not least, a box of peculiar brown wads that looked like spit-out chewing tobacco. Merlin picked one up gingerly and sniffed it.

"Dragon treats?" he asked.

"Yes," Gideon said. "My own recipe: rabbit jerky, dried mulberries, and a little dragon mint."

"Ah, yes. Catnip for wyverns."

Merlin picked up the silver lasso and, stretching a length of it between his hands, gave it a sharp tug. He nodded approvingly. "Mermaid's hair?"

"Yes, cut with a little spider's silk."

"Merfolk *do* ask an outrageous price for an ounce of hair combed by the light of the full moon," said Merlin. "If you are not careful, they will try to sell you a lesser grade, combed by the new moon or even in broad daylight. And it's never as strong."

"Never," Gideon agreed.

Next the elder wizard picked up the golden muzzle. "Not gold overlay, I see, but solid gold. Well, you will be interested to learn about a number of improvements since your day—the safety match and the Band-Aid, to name just two—but you were wise to bring along the moonlight rope and the golden bridle. They would have been quite difficult to obtain Here and Now. As for the few remaining items,"—he picked up the sack of medieval coins—"you and I will have to go shopping. But first we must outfit you with some less conspicuous garments. You're liable to see almost anything in Harvard Square, from Sikh turbans to motorcycle leather, but I'm afraid you would still stand out."

Even wizardry couldn't transform a brown wool suit, sized portly, into anything that would have fit Gideon. Instead, Merlin helped the younger wizard select some garments from mail-order catalogs and then cut them out with scissors. Once these were spread out on the desk—a short-sleeved batik shirt in a pattern of hammerhead sharks, khaki walking shorts with a lot of useful-looking pockets, and black canvas sneakers with leather laces—Merlin said "Presto-chango" over them in Wizard's Latin, and the garments themselves appeared, neatly folded and only a little linty with magic.

Everything fit perfectly. Gideon looked at his reflection in the full-length mirror on the back of the closet door and thought he looked very peculiar indeed, but Merlin nodded his approval.

"Your hair's a smidge longer than the current fashion, but you'll do. By the way, I wouldn't get too attached to the clothes. They expire this time tomorrow."

Ouroboros went through the belt loops on the shorts and did his best impression of a snakeskin belt, while Ignus took up residence in the spacious ink chamber of a vintage fountain pen in Gideon's shirt pocket.

"I used to keep a Fire of my own," Merlin explained, "until he moved in with a neon flamingo in a travel agent's window. When he lived with me we found this pen was the best way for him to travel."

Gideon bowed and said, "We are honored."

Merlin returned the bow. "Now, one last thing before we descend to the street. You will have to decide whether or not to button the second-to-last button on that shirt. If you don't, your Adept's owl will show and advertise to any other wizards we meet that you're a member of the Guild."

Gideon was wearing a pendant with the same owl

clutching a crystal ball that adorned Merlin's lapel. He hesitated with his finger on the second-to-last button. "How many other wizards are here in Boss-town?" He still hadn't managed to pronounce it Bos-tun.

"Not nearly as many as there used to be, goodness knows—it's been years since the membership in G.A.W.A. has been high enough to hold a Convocation—but still more than you might think. And it's not so much how *many* as which *ones.* I let my own owl show, it's true, but then no one is looking for me."

It occurred to Gideon that Kobold had already followed him through the bolt-hole by now. He would have used a tracing spell to follow Gideon's wake through time, but chances were he wouldn't exit the bolt-hole in exactly the same spot. But it was virtually certain Kobold was in this When, if not yet in this Where.

"I will leave it buttoned for now."

Merlin nodded and took up the long object of black pleated silk, the collapsible, portable roof called an umbrella.

"Then let us descend."

"I tell you, we are in the wrong Where," said Febrys peevishly, "*and* the wrong When." Her tightly fitting peplum suit and cork-soled platform shoes, all the rage in 1942, were completely impractical for a trek along wet sand. Using a different spell, Kobold had summoned up their clothes from sackcloth and ashes, based on what his crystal ball had revealed to be the current fashions for the When on the other side of the bolt-hole. His crystal ball had apparently developed a slight astigmatism, and as a result, the clothes were more than half a century out of style.

He was wishing he had left the demon behind, but he didn't like to think what would happen if he returned without the wyvern or without Gideon. He had never seen his master, only heard his voice, well disguised by spells. The voice alone made it clear what the price of failure would be.

The demon would prove useful, though he wished he had an imp instead—so much easier to deal with in all ways, and so much better-smelling. Kobold thought about the ways he might spend his reward, once his task was completed and he was back in his own When and Where. Not just one imp, but a matched pair; one of those collapsible pocket cauldrons that reversed from iron to crystal; and a dram or two of unicorn tears, to sweeten his sleep.

But of course his revenge on Gideon would be the sweetest reward of all.

Kobold strode along a few yards ahead, ignoring Febrys's whining and the stares of teenagers in swim trunks and bikinis. The wizard marched through their game of volleyball, over a snoring sunbather, and straight into a sand castle, demolishing it. Its architect, a girl of six, leaped to her feet with an outraged "Hey!", but her mother stopped her, talking to her in a low voice and casting an interested glance after the oddly dressed pair.

Like his demon servant, Kobold was dressed in the height of fashion for the middle of the twentieth century, or so his calculations had told him. He wore a fedora hat, a suit of shiny blue sharkskin fabric, wing-tip shoes, and a short, wide necktie with a pattern of Hawaiian hula dancers. Suddenly, the sea sent a tongue of fizzing foam up over the toes of his wing-tips, wetting his socks. Heedless of the Guild's first commandment—no showy displays of magical powers around mortals unless absolutely necessary—Kobold muttered a spell. The next wave halted in midair. The volleyball players stopped to point and gawk.

A lifeguard perched on a blue-and-white watchtower blew a shrill blast on his whistle.

"Hey, you! This is a state beach. You can't mess with the water like that. Whatever it is you did, undo it right—*ark!*"

With a magical sizzle and pop, the lifeguard had been transformed into a barking seal, with a whistle around its neck and a white stripe of zinc ointment down the center of its whiskered muzzle.

"Ark! Ark! Ark!"

The little girl was hard at work rebuilding her

sand castle. She was scooping out a new moat with a seashell, ignoring the barking seal atop the lifeguard's tower. As chance would have it—and chance does like to have its way—she was a child with unusual parents, and she took unusual happenings in stride.

The little girl's mother looked up from her magazine, narrowing her eyes over the top of her sunglasses, and biting her lower lip. "Come on, Katie. Time to go."

The sand castle was reluctantly abandoned, its moat half dug. Sandy towels were shaken out, and sunscreen and juice boxes and a poseable mermaid doll with lavender hair flew into a canvas tote bag. A smuggled hermit crab, hidden under a shell in Katie's beach pail, was returned to the sea. Katie and her mother struggled up the last grassy dunes to the parking lot, ooching and ouching their way across the last stretch of hot sand.

They stopped by a silver blue minivan with New Jersey plates. Katie's mom fished her car keys out of the pocket of her shorts. The keys swung from a small owl clutching a crystal ball.

Katie was all buckled in to the backseat when her mother remembered something. She turned and, with her pointer finger, drew a complicated sign in the air in the direction of the lifeguard's tower, adding a quick spell in Wizard's English (approved in the Miami Convocation of 1973).

As the minivan pulled out of the parking lot, the

wave Kobold had halted with a spell completed its downward arc, and the speechless lifeguard, restored to his human form, was left staring down the beach, shaking his head as though he had a water bubble in one ear.

It was late afternoon by the time Mikko and Theodora got back to Cambridge. They made a stop in Central Square.

"I'm going into the co-op to get a few things," said Mikko. "Why don't you go into the art and crafts store and look around? I'll meet you in the paint department."

Theodora went into the arts and crafts store thinking that Mikko was pretty sneaky. In the paint department they had a magnifying glass that clamped on to the edge of a table and lit up and swiveled around. It was pretty expensive, and after calculating how much allowance it would gobble up and deciding she might have to use her birthday checks from Aunt Jane and Aunt Mariah, Theodora contented herself with an extra fine sable brush, and two tiny pots of paint in Krishna blue and sari pink. As she was paying for them Mikko came up with a plastic grocery sack in each hand.

"Ready?"

Theodora nodded. They went out the big doors onto the sidewalk and into the crush of people. Theodora was about to take one of the grocery bags for the walk to the car when Mikko spoke up.

"Wait a sec, Dodo. You've got something stuck to your shoe. Hold your foot up."

Mikko reached down to peel the thin object from the bottom of Theodora's sneaker. But instead of throwing the ticket away, she stood looking down at it in amazement.

"Dodo," she said in a funny voice. "What is it?"

It was definitely *not* a lottery ticket. It wasn't even made of cardboard. What it was was a playing card, painted in jewel-like colors, showing a black wyvern arching its back at a small, purple imp it had chased into a corner. You could tell by just looking at it that the card was very, very old. Theodora felt a shiver run the length of her spine.

"It's my last wyvern card," she said.

6

A Perfectly Good Substitute for Eye of Newt

MERLIN O'SHEA STOOD in the middle of Harvard Yard, his brown tweed coat draped over one arm, revealing red suspenders stretched like bungee cords over his considerable girth. His shirtsleeves were rolled up to the elbow, and the shirt itself was spotted with perspiration. Merlin's face was almost as red as his suspenders, and his eyes had a slightly wild look to them. He stabbed the air with his umbrella in the direction of a tree that was casting a patch of shade.

"There! An oasis." He struck out toward it at a

stumble, and Gideon, whose own shirt was magically free of sweat, followed.

When they were settled on the lawn beneath the tree, Merlin panted, "Now, where's that water?"

Gideon passed him the plastic bottle. Merlin took just a few swallows—he really preferred tea as a beverage—then dampened his handkerchief and draped it over his face with a sigh. He lifted one corner of the handkerchief and peered out balefully.

"We have shopped and I have dropped," he said mournfully. "In the olden days, before the Gap and its ilk took root in Harvard Square, you really *could* find a decent substitute for eye of newt. Not to mention real galoshes and gentleman's handkerchiefs."

Checking to make sure none of the students walking past was looking their way, Gideon let Ouroboros slither out of his belt loops and into the cool grass. Then he cast a spell that slowly and subtly enlarged the shade under their tree, as though someone had spilled a large bucket of shadow-black right where they sat. Anyone looking very closely at it would have thought it a very odd shade indeed, though the spell had another bit in it just to keep anyone from looking very closely. Then he retrieved from his satchel the fruits of their morning's quest: a jar of extralarge stuffed olives from Cardullo's, a fake eyeball encased in a plastic ice cube from the joke shop, and an assortment of vaguely ocular beads from Beadworks.

None of them really looked like newt's eyes.

Gideon shook his head. "I do not believe these will work, Merlin."

"No," the other wizard said from beneath the handkerchief. "Nor do I, really. They are, as the saying goes, a stretch."

They hadn't done much better with the basilisk feather—just a plastic bag of dyed chicken feathers from the crafts store and a single, glossy black flight feather from a crow that Ouroboros's sharp eyes (all four of them) had spotted in front of John Harvard's statue.

They had done better with the medieval coins. They had gone to see a man in a tiny office up a flight of narrow stairs over the movie theater. He had gotten quite flustered when he saw the three coins Gideon had held out to him and had paid handsomely for them. In his new nylon and Velcro wallet, Gideon now had a number of crisp green bills with the portrait of the wizard Benjamin Franklin on them (in Merlin's change purse of wizard money, Franklin was honored on a silver coin, much smaller than a penny, called a "mewlet.") "A notable American patriot and inventor," Merlin explained, "but after all, only a minor wizard. What he's most remembered for is a pamphlet he wrote on the natural history of biddable fire." But all the dollars in the world could not purchase what did not exist, here in the year 2002.

"What if we attempt the Fetching anyway?" Gideon asked.

Merlin removed the handkerchief. His face looked less like a tomato but not any more cheerful.

"We run the risk of fetching something else: a Komodo dragon from the Miami Zoo or someone's pet iguana. Or worse, fetching only *part* of Wycca. You might end up with just her beak or the tip of her tail or some random bits in between."

Gideon shuddered.

"But cheer up, my good fellow. There is one more hunting ground where we might find our quarry. Gather up old Robbie"—this was Merlin's nickname for Ouroboros—"and fish out that subway pass I gave you. The fellow in the booth might catch on if you charm the turnstile again."

Wycca, too, had spent her morning hunting. Moving and redecorating had been exhausting, and she hadn't eaten since her journey through the bolt-hole. Leaving her egg well camouflaged under a layer of peregrine down, she had struck out on a foraging run. She flew high enough that anyone looking up would have seen what would have looked like a large gull, if she was near the water, or else a bird of prey. When she was forced to fly closer to the ground, she took on some of the hue of the sky by ruffling her scales to flash their mirror-like undersides. It was a skill called "minnowing," and Wycca was very good at it, having practiced for many summer afternoons driving the king's hawks wild in a game of invisible tag.

Wycca rejected the bustling stalls selling fish and vegetables at Haymarket—it would have been easy pickings but a little too conspicuous. And she didn't feel much like fighting seagulls for fish off the boats at the pier. Wyverns have a keen sense of smell, and Wycca followed hers across the river to a large castle, the towers of which belched clouds of curiously fragrant steam.

It was the start of the second shift at the New England Confectionary Company. The head confectioner had checked and approved the enormous vats of fondant and nougat and best-quality enrobing semisweet, and with a nod to the foreman on duty, the switch was thrown and vast candy-making apparatuses began stamping out hundreds and hundreds of chocolates with chewy centers. An intense chocolate aroma began to waft from the tall chimneys and out over the surrounding Cambridge neighborhood.

Wycca had paused on the great dome of the main building of the Massachusetts Institute of Technology, snuffling deeply to sample the delicious cloud. What a marvelous, mouthwatering scent! She had no idea what it was, but it certainly smelled good enough to eat.

The castle from which the smell was issuing did not

have the usual fortifications—it had no moat, no arrow slits in the walls, and no crenellations from which defenders might pour boiling oil on besieging armies—but despite the lack of defenses, Wycca did not see a likely way in. There was a smallish door, from which people were exiting and others entering, making signs of greeting to one another. On the other side of the castle, a larger entrance was busy with men lifting boxes into the back of a large wheeled barn with NECCO emblazoned on the side.

Necco must be some kind of magical word, like *Abracadabra,* Wycca thought. Though she had learned to recognize a few written words, she did not possess the power of speech. It was a pity. The magic word might have gained her entrance to the source of the tantalizing aroma.

But there on the roof was the opening she sought. Wycca perked up. She had wriggled though spaces narrower than *that* back at her own castle. The wyvern spread her wings and sailed through the air, alighting on the roof of the factory next to the chimney with NECCO painted on it, too, in huge letters.

The exhaust vent was a snug fit, and when she emerged out the other end, she was missing a few scales. (Luckily, none ended up in packages of Necco wafers.) The smell was overpowering here, but still she could not identify its source. The deafening clatter of the equipment frightened her, and she snapped her beak at a couple of dangling hoses, causing them to hiss and spit steam at her. Arching her back like a terrified cat, Wycca hissed back, then lunged and bit a fat bundle of multi-colored cables in two.

With flashing lights and a chorus of alarms, the state-of-the-art robotized confectionery equipment, which had been installed only the year before, ground to a halt. The safety shutdown system kicked in, and to prevent the expensive equipment from overloading, a trapdoor opened in the assembly line and all the chocolates exiting the molding room dropped into a temporary holding bin.

Which was where Wycca happened to be. She squawked in surprise as she was pelted with thousands of Deluxe Choco-Creams with Cherry Fondant Centers. The scent of warm chocolate enveloped her, more marvelous even than dragon mint.

That was how the wyvern discovered that she adored—nay, worshipped—the heavenly substance sacred to the Aztecs as *tchocoatl* and known to us as chocolate.

Merlin and Gideon and his two companions had traveled the length and breadth of Boston's Chinatown, visiting every tiny grocery and large supermarket and every mom-and-pop Chinese pharmacy, where boxes of dried ginseng root shared counter space with Hong Kong action videos.

In the last pharmacy Gideon looked around and for the first time that day felt at home. It resembled the large apothecary shops he had known in his own time. One wall of the shop was taken up by a vast cabinet, with hundreds of wooden drawers the size of shoe boxes reaching to the ceiling, each labeled in Chinese. A young aproned assistant wheeled a step stool to the appointed spot and handed down to the herbalist drawers full of lotus root and cassia bark. A wall chart showed other traditional medicines made out of silkworm cocoons, cicada husks, seashells, even dried scorpions. The herbalist, a middle-aged Chinese woman, worked at the metal counter weighing out portions in a scale with brass weights and wrapping remedies up in paper parcels.

They had to wait while she explained a remedy to a young mother who had a fussy baby in a stroller. But at last it was their turn.

Chinese was one of Merlin's languages, and he and the herbalist had a long conversation, with much gesturing, in Mandarin. Merlin did a lot of nodding "yes" and the herbalist did a lot of shaking her head "no." Eventually she consulted a few large books, then disappeared through a curtain into a back room.

She was gone for some time, and while they waited the assistant brought them a dish of salty-sweet preserved plums and small porcelain cups of green tea. At length the herbalist reappeared, clutching an old mayonnaise jar full of murky liquid. In it floated a sinister object, slightly oval and mottled green and black, like a thousand-year-old poached egg. She held the jar out to Merlin, still shaking her head and speaking rapidly in Mandarin. Every time he reached to take the jar from her, she would pull it back and there would be another burst of Mandarin. It seemed to Gideon that Merlin was being scolded.

Merlin turned to Gideon, holding out the jar and making a face. "This is *long yian,* eye of the dragon. She says it is the closest thing she has. It is very old and powerful, and we must be very careful with it."

The herbalist produced a piece of paper, again in Chinese, and Merlin initialed it in two places and then signed it.

"I've just absolved her of any responsibility and promised not to sue her for malpractice."

"Malpractice?" Gideon repeated, puzzled.

Ouroboros consulted his forward memory. "After your time. A legal innovation of the seventeenth century," he whispered.

Several portraits of Benjamin Franklin changed hands, and the herbalist was now all smiles. As Gideon and Merlin went out the door, she called after them, "Thank you! Please come again."

—ʍʍ—

The Oglethorpe kitchen had been transformed into an operating room. An old sheet had been thrown over the kitchen table, and the swiveling desk lamp had been borrowed from Mr. Oglethorpe's office. At one end of the table an array of tiny sponges, brushes, and metal spatulas was laid out on a dishtowel next to a row of small bottles. Mikko was bent over the object on the table with a magnifying glass, and from time to time Theodora would hand her a different tool or the tiny bottle of mineral spirits. At last Mikko sat back and let out a long breath.

"I always knew that class in art restoration would come in handy some day," she said. "Now take a look, Dodo, and tell me what you think."

Theodora pressed close to see. Sometimes she wondered if there was anything Mikko hadn't taken a class in. Most of them seemed to have to do with art or rare books and Theodora knew Mikko had very nearly become a professor of art history.

Now that the grime from the streets of Central Square had been carefully cleaned away, the thin ivory card seem to glow with color. The red-eyed, purple imp recoiled from the lunging wyvern, its clawlike hands held up in a defensive gesture and its features twisted into a snarl of fear. The wyvern itself gleamed iridescent blue-black along its back, where its closely set scales took on the gloss of a seal's pelt. Its wings were folded back, but you could see that they were membranous, like a bat's, and so thin in places that the light shone through. Its wickedly sharp beak was silvery black, like a gun muzzle, and its eyes were the brightest green. The curled ribbon of its forked tongue, as it lashed out at the cornered imp was vividly scarlet. (Real wyverns' tongues are neither scarlet nor forked, but that does not enter into this story.)

The cleaning had also revealed details along the margin of the card not visible when Mikko had peeled it from the bottom of Theodora's shoe. The wyvern wore a golden collar, to which was attached a thin silver cable, pulled taut. You could just see, on the very edge of the card, the thumb and fingers of a hand holding tightly to the other end of the cable. There was a glimpse of the hem of a black tunic and the curled scarlet tip of a shoe.

Theodora looked up, her eyes shining.

"Oh, Mikko," she said, "isn't it magic?"

7

A Talent for Trouble

WYCCA SAT ON the roof of the dome at the Massachusetts Institute of Technology, licking the last of the cherry fondant from between her toes. Her belly was so swollen with chocolate, she looked like she was still carrying her egg. Every time she exhaled she let loose a hot cloud of burnt-sugar vapor. Through her veins coursed a dangerous mixture that was one-quarter dragon's blood and three-quarters sugar and caffeine. The wyvern was wired, her normal impishness cranked up to a dangerous pitch. She would have to work off the energy somehow.

She made her way over to the Boston Public

Gardens, fully intending to dive-bomb the tourists on the swan boats and harass the real swans dabbling among the rushes. No sooner had she found a hiding place among the roots of a tree from which to plot her mischief, than she was distracted by a sudden commotion in her mind, and a writhing in the shadows nearby.

The wyvern flattened her body to the ground and laid her ears close to her head. This was not a bolt-hole, and no magic she knew, wild or tame or anywhere in between. Once when she had been a young wyvern in training, Gideon had bade her sit beside the fire while he unlocked a chest and removed a squat iron bottle bound with seven elvish harp strings. When the last strand had been unwound, the wizard had drawn the cork and waved the bottle under Wycca's snout and then hastily recorked it, wound it back up in the seven long silver threads, and returned the bottle to its chest. The chest waddled back to its shelf on clawed feet. Wycca had coughed and pawed at her snout, shaking her head as if to shake the memory of the smell out of it.

"I cannot say the word for it aloud," Gideon had said. "But it is magic turned in on itself—magic turned rabid and foul. Now you know the smell of it. If you ever chance on it, don't approach. Return to me immediately."

As Wycca watched, the commotion in her brain ceased and the writhing in the shadows slipped away, a fluid darkness sliding down a storm drain. When it had gone, Wycca no longer wanted to harass the swans. She couldn't return to Gideon, but she could go back to her nest and her egg, and that is what she did.

Mikko and Theodora were fighting. Mikko was standing with her back to the kitchen sink, looking tired and worn out. The tarot card was still on the kitchen table.

"Look, Dodo, you know if your father were here he wouldn't let you keep it. It's obviously old and rare and valuable. Someone's probably looking for it, and even if we can't locate its rightful owner, it belongs in a museum where it can be taken care of properly and where people can come and see it."

Theodora was sitting on the kitchen stool, her arms folded across her chest, her face twisted into a dark glower. She had an awful, heavy feeling in her chest, like she was going to explode. She couldn't look Mikko straight in the eye, but she kept darting poisonous glances her way.

"Well, he isn't here. *I* found it—it was on the bottom of *my* shoe. You can't make me give it back. And don't call me Dodo! I hate it when you call me that. My dad is allowed to call me that, but you're not." Even if this had been true (which it wasn't) it was incredibly bratty to say, and Theodora blushed as she said it.

Now Mikko looked sad as well as tired. "Well, I thought you hated being called Theodora more. I'm sorry, I can't look the other way and pretend this is okay. It's wrong. And I'm sorry you can't realize that you don't always have to own something to enjoy it."

Theodora stormed off to her room to sulk. She flipped through her pile of wyvern holo-comics without really reading them, rearranged her other wyvernalia, and played the new *Orcs & Omens* cartridge for her GameBot. At last she realized it was eight o'clock and Mikko hadn't called her for dinner.

There was light under the door to Mikko's room, and she could hear Mikko's TV, tuned to an old movie. The kitchen was dark and there was no sign of any dinner. The sheet had been removed from the kitchen table, and all the cleaning implements and small brown bottles were put away, but the tarot card was still there, in the center of the table, with a note from Mikko.

All it said was:

Theodora,

Whatever you decide to do with this tomorrow, it still needs to dry tonight. Please leave it where it is.

Mikko

Next to the note were two postcards. The first had a picture of a cowboy riding a bucking bronco, with the banner WILD CALGARY. The second showed a range of purple, misty mountains beneath the words GREETINGS

FROM THE ADIRONDACKS. There was no card from Laos—it was too soon to expect one, anyway.

She read Valerie's card first. As usual, Val had made the maximum use of the available space, writing right up to the edge of the stamp. The back of the card was covered in her microscopic printing. Val had insanely teeny writing; in fourth grade she had written little books that folded up and fit inside walnut shells. Her news was all of the "Help, I'm being held prisoner in a music camp" variety, with details about the warden, guards, "food," and fellow inmates. Milo's card made it clear that he was having a great time in Calgary, going fossil-hunting and camping and fishing with his new stepdad.

Neither card cheered her up any, and for some reason Milo's card made her feel worse. Theodora went into the pantry and made a triple-decker peanut butter, Marshmallow Fluff, and banana sandwich, which she washed down with chocolate milk.

When she had finished she stood in the kitchen, drinking her second glass of milk and thinking. The kitchen light seemed to fall like a spotlight on the tarot card, making the purple imp glow.

The real estate agent unlocked the door to the penthouse apartment in Emerald Towers, overlooking the Boston Public Gardens. The rent on the apartment was more than ten thousand dollars a month, and she was nearly dizzy with the thought of her commission. But she had to admit to herself she did not care for the prospective tenants.

Since the incident on the beach in New Jersey, Kobold and Febrys had traded their 1940s attire for more appropriate clothing: an Italian suit for Mr. Lambton (as he was calling himself Here and Now) and a chic ensemble for Ms. Worm, who had cut her hair fashionably short and was wearing green contact lenses to give her demon eyes a more human appearance.

The two of them gave the real estate agent the creeps. But she could smell a deal, and she reminded herself that this would put her in the running for Agent of the Month and maybe even Agent of the Year. She picked up a sleek white remote control from the hall table.

"You'll see that everything is controlled by the central computer." She pressed some buttons on the remote and the lights came on, then dimmed, then brightened. She pressed different buttons and the silk drapes opened and closed; a panel slid open in the wall to reveal a row of bottles and glasses. Yet another button and a flat screen television screen came on showing a golf tournament.

"It's a prototype," she said. "This model isn't even in general production yet."

Mr. Lambton held his hand out for the remote and

pressed the buttons cautiously, looking at the screen with intense interest as the tournament changed to show a close-up of a bottle containing an effervescent potion, which delirious youths consumed with gusto. He pressed another button and the sparkling potion was replaced by a group of enthralled children dancing in a ring around a lumpen effigy of a dragon. Ms. Worm stared at the screen and smiled in a way that even the real estate agent thought unnatural.

"We'll take it," said Mr. Lambton. From his inner jacket pocket he produced a pen and a checkbook in a fancy leather cover and swiftly wrote out a check. He handed it to the agent, who raised her eyebrows at the sum he had written and tried to explain that there were some formalities; his references would have to be checked first and a lease drawn up. But a spell from the wizard soon led her train of thought astray, and furrowing her brow, the agent dropped the keys to the penthouse on the hall table and wandered out the door.

Kobold waved his hand and the door closed behind the retreating agent. He glanced around the room's furnishings—all softly gleaming leather, wood, steel, and glass, a far cry from his usual accommodations, with moth-eaten bed curtains, freezing flagstones, fleas in the mattress, and mice in the walls. When his task was done here, it would be very difficult to leave, even with a reward waiting for him on the other end of the bolt-hole, back in his own When and Where. But he knew that if he did not return with Wycca, and proof of his mission accomplished, something worse than another wizard might be sent through the bolt-hole after him. Kobold felt, and not for the first time, a pang of misgiving about his master, whose face he had never seen and whose name he had never heard. He was deep in thought when he caught sight of the demon.

For a moment, he had forgotten about her. Now he frowned.

Febrys had kicked off her high heels and was rubbing her sore, cloven feet. Her mortal form was a cheap replica of a human woman, and the spellwork was especially shoddy around the feet. (It takes a really good wizard to do toes.)

"I would not want to be a human woman here," she said. "And I do not like contact lenses."

"Well, you don't have to like them. Now go practice your smile while I get to work."

When the demon had gone into the powder room to practice smiling in the mirror, the wizard stood looking out across the Public Garden at the brownstones of Back Bay.

They were out there somewhere, Gideon and his wyvern. Kobold murmured a single word.

"Soon."

8

An Unfortunate Fortune

HIGH ABOVE THE harbor Wycca lay on her nest and whined. Her underbelly scales were scraped from the tumbles through the factory chute, her stomach was uncomfortably stretched from her chocolate binge, and now that the sugar and caffeine were wearing off she could just feel the beginnings of a terrible headache.

But even through the haze of chocolate the wyvern's maternal instincts were strong. Wycca lifted her aching head and used her beak to conduct her hourly inspection of the egg. Running the sensitive tip of her beak lightly all over its surface, she assured herself that there were no cracks in the shell. She listened closely for the faint *wroa-wroa* that was a wyvern's equivalent of a hatching chick's *peep-peep.* The egg was perfectly whole, the hatchling inside silent. Satisfied, Wycca tucked the nesting material close around the egg and settled herself on it as best she could.

Soon she was asleep, her scaled feet twitching in a wyvern's dream of chocolate.

When Merlin awakened from his nap it was just ten o'clock. He roused Gideon, and they paused for a meal of food summoned magically all the way from China. Merlin took the food, handed the courier money, and sent him back to China. Gideon thought it was a powerful spell indeed, if a slow one: It had taken the Chinese man and the food twenty-five minutes to make the journey from the bottom of the world, hardly the blink of an eye.

From white paper boxes with metal handles, Merlin produced steaming hot fowl stewed with spices, and rice, which they ate with sticks. Afterward they ate small pastries that you broke open to see the fortune sealed inside. (Much more humane, Gideon thought, than the king's old habit of sealing fortune-tellers inside giant pies for the amusement of the court.)

Merlin wiped his mouth with a paper napkin.

"Now, we had better get to work. It's almost midnight."

The hours before dawn are the ideal window for conducting a Fetching, and working together, it would take them nearly three hours to assemble the equipment and prepare for the full form of the Fetching ceremony.

From under his four-poster bed, Merlin pulled a long, flat box, marked all over with wizardly runes and the words ABSOLUTELY NOT TO BE OPENED BY ANYONE WITHOUT THE EXPRESS PERMISSION OR SUPERVISION OF IAIN MERLIN O'SHEA, PH.D., ADEPT OF THE WIZARDLY ARTS.

The box held a long cable made of spun glass wrapped in silver. Suspended every seven inches along its length was a short glass tube, open at one end and pointed at the other. There were also dozens of silver clips resembling curtain hooks. Back in the study Merlin spread everything out on the carpet and sighed.

"You would think one of the Convocations would have come up with a simpler way to fetch a wyvern. The Committee on Fetchings has been meeting for three hundred years without anything to show for it."

Merlin had to inspect each of the 101 tubes along the length of the cable for cracks; if he found one, the tube had to be replaced with a new one from a wooden box with an Edinburgh postmark. Then every tube had to be struck with a tiny silver hammer, while Merlin listened to the pitch. If the pitch was off, it had to be adjusted by polishing the rim of the glass tube with an emery cloth. Then the whole cord had to be gone over, to see if the silver wrapping was frayed anywhere, and rubbed with a silk buffing cloth moistened with oil from a tiny oilcan. After an hour on his hands and knees doing this, Merlin straightened with a groan and hobbled into the kitchen to make a pot of coffee.

Gideon's task was just as tedious. On each of 101 tiny slips of parchment, each a little larger than a fortune-cookie fortune, he was writing out, in the smallest possible hand, in scarlet ink to which he had added drops of his own blood, sweat, and tears, words that it would be a breach of the Wizard's Code to repeat. They had lots of I's to dot and T's to cross; and even in Wizard's English, it was very tiresome to write 101 times on impossibly tiny pieces of paper. When the ink had dried Gideon had to roll up each spell and tie it with silver thread.

Gideon accepted a cup of coffee and winced at the strange, bitter brew. But Merlin urged him to finish it and he did.

It was nearly three in the morning. With the use of the silver hooks, the glass cable with its dangling tubes had been strung around the study just below the ceiling. Gideon opened his satchel and took out the golden bridle and the silver cable of mermaid's hair.

In the middle of the room, in the center of the circle formed by the glass cable, Merlin had set up an electric hot plate and a copper double boiler. A copper cauldron suspended directly over a fire of alder wood was traditional, but in the long form of a Fetching a few modern contrivances were allowed, and Merlin was doing everything he could to avoid attracting the attention of his nosy neighbor in apartment 3B. Just to be safe, he removed the battery from the smoke alarm.

Into the top of the double boiler went a teacupful of honey and another of wine, as well as a bottle of witch hazel from the drugstore (witch-hazel wood being preferred by dowsers for finding lost things). Merlin sprinkled in some toad's eyelashes from a small metal tin that had once held Italian licorice, and Gideon added one of Wycca's scales.

Merlin went over to the stereo and put on a recording of chanting in Wizard's Latin. "There is a small record company here in North Cambridge that puts out a few titles on the G.A.W.A. label," he explained. "And the chanting can get so tiresome."

The dragon's eye and its putrid liquid were added to the bubbling cauldron, and both wizards coughed and gagged at the terrible smell.

"Skunk and saltpeter! What a stink!" cried Merlin. "Do you have our basilisk feather?"

Gideon drew from his pocket a gaudy feather from a Chinese pheasant, also procured on their trip to Chinatown. This he placed not in the cauldron, but on the fire itself. A rank smell filled the room.

"Worse and worse!" cried Merlin, holding his nose. "But here—something's wrong. The glass isn't ringing."

Once the basilisk feather was added to the fire, the glass tubes holding the 101 spells were supposed to begin ringing in tune with the chanting. Merlin did a quick check and discovered one glass tube was missing its tiny paper scroll.

"There, on the floor by the chair," he said, pointing.

The pheasant feather was nearly consumed. Gideon grabbed the slip of paper and quickly tied it up with a piece of silver thread.

As soon as the 101st spell was safely in its glass tube, a loud tone, like the sound made when you wet your finger and run it along the rim of a drinking glass, rose from the glass circle of spells. Merlin put on his red chanting cap and took out a small, red leather book with G.A.W.A. POCKET CHANTER on the spine in gold, and he and Gideon began adding their voices to the chanting coming from the stereo. Thick black smoke began to rise from the double boiler, filling the room. It was magical, more like cool steam than smoke, so it did not sting their eyes or make them choke.

The smoke began to solidify, forming edges, then surfaces, then forms recognizable as limbs, wings, a snout, and a tail. Gideon stopped chanting. Something was very wrong. The form was far too large for a wyvern and not at all the right shape. It was not any dragon shape he had ever seen. The head was too large, the body too long.

Merlin looked up from his Pocket Chanter to ask Gideon why he had stopped chanting. But he only gaped at the thing they had fetched.

It was a kind of dragon, to be sure. You have probably seen one, or an imitation of one, if you have ever been to a Chinese New Year's celebration, with firecrackers and dancers in dragon costumes. This was that sort of dragon, but there were no dancers hidden inside its long, scaly body. It was a *ying-long,* a Chinese five-toed imperial dragon. It had a camel's head adorned with stag's antlers, tiger's paws clawed with eagle's talons, and a long, serpentine body covered with brilliant scales that shone like red and gold enamel. It snorted at them through enormous nostrils and stared at them with eyes the size of headlights.

Gideon reached with trembling fingers for the glass tube that held the 101st spell. He took out the scroll and unrolled it. With a groan of dismay, he handed it to Merlin.

It did not have a spell in Wizard's English written in Gideon's blood, sweat, and tears. It was a fortune-cookie fortune. All it said in faded red printing was:

☺ Something lost will be restored to you. ☺
Your lucky numbers are 8, 38, 40, 42, and 75.

Merlin smiled a crooked smile. "No wonder we summoned up a Chinese dragon."

Someone began pounding on the apartment door. A muffled voice came to them through the steel and wood.

"Professor O'Shea? It's the super, Mr. Mufti. We've had a report of toxic fumes coming from this apartment. A fireman is with me."

"Please open the door, Professor O'Shea," said another, deeper voice. "Otherwise we'll have to break it down."

"Actually, I have a passkey," said Mr. Mufti's voice.

"I'll be right there!" Merlin shouted. Under his breath he hissed to Gideon, "Quick, get your hands on the back end of this creature and *push!*"

"Push where?" asked Gideon, casting his eyes around the study for a place to conceal the dragon.

"Into the bathroom! We'll have to stuff it into the tub! Now, heave!"

9

A Dragon in the Bathtub

"THE FORTUNATE THING about Chinese dragons," said Merlin in between *oofs* and *args,* "is that they are really quite agreeable creatures."

The *ying-long* was wedged in the narrow doorway to the bathroom. Merlin and Gideon were pushing it with all their might, which was not easy: the scales were quite slippery and the dragon itself ticklish. It rolled over in the doorway and exposed its vast belly for scratching.

"No, no, no!" cried Merlin. "Ying, old thing, this is no time for a tummy tickle. Gideon, climb over him and try pulling on his other end."

Gideon slid up and over the scaly body and considered where to grab on to the dragon's head. At last he seized it by its short, straight horns.

"I have hold of it."

"Now, on the count of three: one, two . . . *thrrreee!*"

With a sound like an enormous cork popping, the dragon shot out of the doorway and into the bathroom, its claws scrabbling wildly on the tiles, coming to a stop against the side of the tub with a violent *thump* that caused plaster to rain down from the bathroom ceiling.

Merlin turned on the shower full blast. The *ying-long* immediately clambered over the edge of the tub to get under the spray, it being a watery kind of dragon that liked to keep wet. Its coils filled the tub and flowed over it, and its head rose over the shower-curtain rod. It blinked contentedly at them with its huge eyes.

"Now stay in here," Merlin said to Gideon, "and sing at the top of your lungs."

"Sing?"

"Yes! The dance hits from 1273. Whatever ditties the lute players were playing when you left. Just so they don't hear our friend here." Merlin closed the door.

Gideon sat down on the lid of the toilet and cleared his throat. Then he began to warble in a nervous tenor:

"When the sweet bree-eeze turns bit-ter,
And the leaf fa-ah-alls from the bra-anch . . ."

When Merlin exited the bathroom, Mr. Mufti was just opening the apartment door with the passkey. Merlin could see his overinterested neighbor, Mrs. Wigglesworth from apartment 3B, hovering in the hallway. As the door was opened, the cloud of fetching smoke, redolent of rotten eggs and gunpowder, flowed out into the hallway. Mrs. Wigglesworth gave a shriek and retreated to the safety of her apartment.

The fireman and the super stood and stared at the fetching equipment set up in the study. The wizard-chant recording had been set to repeat, and Merlin hastily waved a hand in the direction of the stereo. The chanting stopped.

The fireman carefully examined the wiring on the hot plate, then inspected the glass cable strung along the ceiling.

"This isn't electric—what does it do?"

"It's part of a Shinto religious ceremony. An offering to my ancestors," said Merlin, kicking the golden bridle and moonlight rope under the sofa.

"But what's all the rest of this?" The fireman waved a hand to indicate the copper double boiler and hot plate.

"Part of a demonstration for a class I'm teaching on comparative folklore. It's a re-creation, with modern adjustments, of a medieval apparatus for summoning a dragon."

"Really!" said the fireman, taking out a small wire-bound notepad and flipping to a blank page. "Tell me more."

"Well, people in the thirteenth century believed a great many strange things," said Merlin, "and one of the things they believed was that wise men—'wizards,' if you will—could brew potions and chant spells that would summon dragons and other magical creatures out of the ether."

"Fascinating," said the fireman, scribbling on his notepad. "Now, what exactly was in this brew of yours?"

"Oh, a nice French burgundy, some clover honey, and witch hazel," said Merlin. "According to the ancient manuscripts, we should really have added eye of newt, but you can't really go to the local drugstore and pick up that kind of thing, can you?"

Mr. Mufti and the fireman laughed. Merlin joined in, laughing a little too loudly.

"Now, Professor O'Shea," said the fireman. "You said *we*. '*We* should really have added eye of newt.' Was someone else here performing this midnight ceremony with you?"

"Yes, a former graduate student—a foreign exchange student, you might say—who's staying with me. He's in the shower at the moment."

As if on cue, another chorus of "When the Sweet Breeze Turns Bitter" wafted to them from under the bathroom door. By now the *ying-long* was joining in with a high, wordless keening like a dog howling along to the high notes of "The Star-Spangled Banner."

"Uh-huh," said the fireman, making more notes. "Well, the next time you want to summon any dragons, make sure you do it in a well-ventilated area."

"There won't be a next time," said Mr. Mufti, giving Merlin a meaningful look.

After further assurances to Mr. Mufti that the dragon ceremony would not be repeated, whether or not it was a violation of the building's no-pets policy, Merlin closed the door firmly behind them.

Gideon emerged from the bathroom, his hair and clothes clinging to him from the steam.

"A narrow escape. I was running out of verses," he said. "And the *ying-long* was beginning to get waterlogged."

Merlin was too exhausted from their adventure for his usual nightcap of cocoa and crossword. He took two sleeping tablets instead and switched on an electronic device on his nightstand that mimicked the sound of ocean waves. Through the open doorway Gideon could see Merlin's head on the pillow, eyes shielded from stray light by a padded satin eye mask.

Gideon slipped out of his clothes—the magical ones that were due to expire in a few hours, anyway—and into an extralarge Harvard nightshirt purchased in the square. He stretched out under the blankets and, as he was dropping off to sleep, made a sign in the air to ward off dreams, good and bad alike, wishing his special eye drops for ensuring sweet sleep (magically compounded from the whiskers of dormice) weren't in his nightstand at home.

Theodora was having a restless night. It might have been the triple-decker sandwich, or it might have been the second glass of chocolate milk. It might even have been a teensy-weensy bit of guilty conscience. But Theodora didn't spend a lot of time wondering. At three o'clock she threw off the covers and got out of bed.

She took her quilt and her pillow and went into the living room. Her DVD of *Wizards & Wyverns* was already in the player, so she made herself a nest on the sofa and settled in to watch.

But right in the middle of her favorite scene—Jura, the young female wyvernkeeper, rescuing the wounded baby wyvern—Theodora realized she was bored. She channel-surfed past two pro wrestling matches, a Cantonese soap opera, an infomercial for a psychic dating service for pets, and an old Godzilla movie, then turned the TV off. It was still only a quarter after four.

She got up to check on the tarot card. The wyvern and imp were still there in the middle of the kitchen table, next to Mikko's note. Theodora reached out and felt the card gingerly. Because it was painted on thin ivory and not cardboard, it was already completely dry.

Technically, she *had* left it where it was until "tomorrow." This was tomorrow. It had been tomorrow for four hours and fifteen minutes already. And she wasn't actually going to *take* the card, just borrow it for about ten minutes and put it right back.

As she picked the card up she suddenly remembered a Christmas when she had gone into the living room to inspect the presents while her parents were still asleep. Mrs. Oglethorpe had heard a noise and come downstairs to find a five-year-old Theodora in the middle of all her opened presents. Her mom hadn't yelled or anything; she just swore Theodora to secrecy and sent her back to bed. When they all came downstairs around 8:15, Theodora's presents were once again piled under the tree, done up in paper and ribbon just as if nothing had happened. Theodora did her best to act completely surprised as she opened every gift for the second time.

But this isn't going to be like that! she snapped at her conscience.

She went into her dad's study and hit the switch on the surge protector into which everything was plugged. The computer, printer, and scanner all came to life, with *beeps* and *zrrrps* and *whirrs*, much louder in the silent house than she had expected. She listened for the sound of Mikko's door opening, but there was nothing but the low drone of the fan inside the computer.

Theodora set the card facedown on the scanner and started up the scanning software. The printer had only plain white paper in it, but in the bottom drawer of her dad's desk she found some heavy ivory paper, marbled to look like parchment, left over from a history project on the Middle Ages.

For some reason, her heart was thudding in her chest. Maybe it was the fear of discovery—not only had she taken the card, she was using her dad's computer without permission—but it might just have been excitement and anticipation. If this worked, she knew something wonderful would happen, and not just joining the Wyvernkeeper's Circle.

"Oh," she whispered under her breath, her finger poised on the mouse button. "If only it was a real wyvern."

She clicked on SCAN, and the blue scanner light came on and moved from the top of the card to the bottom. A perfect copy of the card appeared, bit by bit, on the monitor in front of Theodora. Lit up on the computer screen, the colors took on new life. The terrified imp looked as though he might hop down from the monitor and take off down the hallway.

Theodora went up into the menu at the top of the

screen and found the PRINT command. She clicked and a few seconds later a sheet of paper slid into the printer tray.

It looked great, even through the paper wasn't quite thick enough. But suddenly she had an even better idea. She ran to her room and, after rummaging in her desk, found a box of special transfer paper for making iron-on designs and a piece of thin, white cardboard.

She had never set up the ironing board before, and it unfolded into position with a loud metallic squeal. Theodora stood petrified, waiting for Mikko's door to fly open and the thud of frantic footsteps in the hall.

There was only a murmured *"Uhhh? Whassat?"* from Mikko's room.

"Nothing," Theodora called back.

"Uhnf," was the muffled reply.

While the iron was warming up Theodora printed the image out again on the iron-on transfer paper. It came out even better this time.

The transfer made a nasty, melting-plastic smell when she was ironing it on, and when it had cooled enough so she could peel the backing away, she thought she heard a tiny little "Eee!" as though the imp were protesting. Theodora got Mikko's good sewing scissors out of the mending basket on the top shelf of the linen closet and carefully cut out the card.

It looked wonderful, almost like the real thing. She admired it for a few minutes, then saw it was seven minutes to six. Mikko always got up at six to do her morning tai chi in the backyard.

Theodora scurried around, putting the iron and ironing board away, sweeping up the paper trimmings, and turning off the computer, printer, and scanner. By 5:57 she was back in bed in her best deep-asleep pose. She peered out above the covers, admiring her new tarot card on her bedside table. It looked great. You almost couldn't tell it apart from the real one.

Theodora sat up in bed. It *was* real. She had taken the real card to her room and had left the *copy* on the kitchen table. It looked good but not that good. Mikko would never be fooled.

At six o'clock sharp Mikko's door opened, and Theodora heard Frankie's morning *"feed me-feed me-feed me"* meow as he padded down the hall ahead of Mikko. There was the sound of the fridge opening and the clink of silverware as Mikko fished a clean fork from the dish drainer, then another anxious meow from Frankie as Mikko tapped the cat food from the fork onto Frankie's dish. Then Theodora heard Mikko turn the dead bolt on the side door and undo the latch on the screen.

Creeping to her window, Theodora could see Mikko in the backyard, beginning her slow-motion martial-arts moves.

Theodora tiptoed to the kitchen. The backyard was right in front of the kitchen window, and depending where she was in her routine, Mikko either faced into the kitchen or away from it. Theodora waited for Mikko to turn her back. Then she dashed to the table, switched the cards, and ran back to the safety of the corner.

This time she was careful to bury the copy deep in the pile of wyvernalia by her window.

10

More Than One Way to Fetch a Wyvern

THERE IS MORE than one way to go about a Fetching. Merlin and Gideon had gone about it the officially sanctioned, G.A.W.A. way, with the elaborate apparatus and the chanting and the eye of newt. But there was another, unsanctioned way to fetch a wyvern, and that was Kobold's way.

A wizard willing to turn his back on the approved spells of the Guild of Adepts in the Wizardly Arts might begin by finding himself a copy of a book banned at the Constantinople Convocation of 1100. *The Book of the New Adept* had been written by a rogue wizard expelled from the Guild back in the 900s. In it he had collected a series of magical shortcuts, banned because they were unstable and dangerous. The book also included dozens of incantations for summoning up things that were really best left unsummoned.

One of the shortcuts the anonymous tenth-century wizard had recorded was an easier way to fetch a wyvern, especially if one wanted to turn that wyvern against its current master. You could say a spell and summon up a Shadow—a reverse copy, like a reflection in a mirror—of the real wyvern. The shadow wyvern would seek out its mirror twin, the copy drawn to the original like metal to a magnet.

The problem was, the Guild of Adepts had done a good job of tracking down and destroying copies of *The Book of the New Adept* (it was, in fact, a job at which wyverns excelled). Kobold had not been able to obtain a copy back in his own time. But he had great hopes for his prospects in twenty-first-century Boston.

On the screen in the living room of the penthouse, he had called up the electronic yellow pages for the city of Boston and had found the category BOOKS, USED & RARE. He wrote down the names of booksellers who specialized in books made before the invention of the printing press and in books on the occult. There were ten names.

Kobold lingered over the list, pursing his lips.

"Ebeneezer Abernathy, Antiquarian Bookseller, on Joy Street," he read aloud. Then he called for his demon.

Febrys hissed in dismay. "I do not want to put on human woman shoes."

But one look from Kobold, and Febrys reached for her high heels with a whimper.

"You look terrible," said Merlin.

"I feel so," Gideon admitted.

The older wizard had returned from an early morning errand to the corner store to find Gideon dressed and in the kitchen. The younger wizard had managed to find the canister of ground coffee in the freezer and figure out how to work the coffeemaker, with a little coaching from Ouroboros.

As Merlin filled his own mug, Gideon explained. "I was much troubled by dreams, even though I made the usual sign to prevent them. I feel my enemy is close by."

"As a matter of fact, I wanted to talk to you about that." Merlin drew from the grocery bag a half-gallon of milk. It looked like a normal milk carton, until you realized that the symbol for the dairy was a winged cow and that there was a tiny owl clutching a crystal ball printed very small under the panel of nutritional information.

Gideon had already learned about the custom of printing the pictures of missing persons on the sides of milk cartons, but his heart sank as he saw who was pictured on the carton of Dreamtime Dairy 2% Milk from Magically Contented Cows.

There on the side panel, under the bold heading WANTED, were police-style sketches of Kobold in his slouch fedora and Febrys in her 1940s hairdo, with the following caption:

> Last observed in the vicinity of Wildwood, New Jersey. Male suspect displayed Level VII Guild powers; female suspect's appearance and demeanor consistent with that of a Demon First Class. Approach with caution. Report sightings immediately to your local G.A.W.A. officer.

"Unfortunately," said Merlin, "this is an election year for the Guild. Our local G.A.W.A. officer is either off campaigning or else lying low, trying to avoid being conscripted to serve as a delegate. The last time I was conscripted, the Convocation lasted seven years. I'm afraid we won't be able to rely on G.A.W.A. to render any practical assistance."

"How distant is Wildwood, New Jersey?" asked Gideon.

"Not distant enough," said Merlin. "Judging from the date on this carton, they've had more than enough time to make their way up the coast to Boston."

"That would explain my dreams." Gideon turned the carton so that he did not have to look at the drawing of Kobold's lined and spiteful countenance. A dream-warding spell could repel only natural dreams, not un-natural ones concocted by sorcery, the kind Kobold had sent through the night air to find Gideon.

Merlin split a sesame bagel and dropped the halves into the slots of the toaster. "Gideon, pardon me for saying this, but Kobold's vendetta does not seem to be adequately explained by the fact that you beat him out for the job as Number One Wizard. Please don't be offended if I say that there must be more behind this than professional rivalry, more than you've been willing to tell your friend Merlin."

Gideon squirmed a little in his chair, like a boy caught in a fib. "Yes. There is more. Kobold is my half brother."

"Aha!" Merlin murmured softly into his coffee.

"When we were sixteen, the year we were both apprenticed to the Sorcerer Royal, there was a maiden—"

"I knew it!" Merlin set his mug down on the table sharply, sending a small tidal wave of coffee over the rim. "I *knew* there was a girl in it somewhere."

Instead of blushing, Gideon went very pale. "I do not care to speak of it, even now." He toyed with the lid of the jam pot. "Gwynlyn was the sorcerer's daughter. Fair, of course—uncommonly fair. But beauty was only one of her charms. She had a keen reason and a sharp wit and a good heart—and a most wonderful way with young dragons."

"And she favored you over Kobold?"

"If it had only been that! We were young, my brother and I, green in the ways of love and green with jealousy. Once jealousy had pushed love aside, it became a contest with Gwynlyn as the prize. In the end, she vowed she would have neither of us."

"And who could blame her? But that was not the end of it."

"No. Even if he was not losing her to me, Kobold could not bear to lose. He had learned just enough sorcery to cast a very dangerous spell. No innocent love charm to slip under her pillow; he stole into the sorcerer's own workroom and took what he needed from a locked cabinet to perform a full-dress love-binding."

A full-dress love-binding was a powerful spell that bound the beloved to the spellcaster with an unbreakable bond, no matter how unwilling the beloved might be. Often the price of its effectiveness was madness. It went against the Wizard's Code and had been banned from quite early on in the Guild's history.

Now it was Merlin's turn to go white. "Was she . . . ? Did she . . . ?"

"She lived, but the spell robbed her of her wits. Her father was able to undo some of the damage and sent her to recover on a distant isle. Kobold was denounced before the court and stripped of his license to work magic."

Merlin could only shake his head. "After such a crime how was he able to make his living, even as a traveling wizard?"

"Seven centuries ago such a disgrace was not the impediment it would be today. To a minor baronet disgraced himself, a defrocked wizard without scruples was a bargain at twice the price."

"And out of his guilt Kobold formed a mad delusion that you were to blame for Gywnlyn's fate?"

A little color had returned to Gideon's face, but his eyes were still full of a far-off sadness. "Yes. For a time I suffered under the same delusion myself."

They had just finished the bagel when there was a low, rumbling yawn from the direction of the bathroom. Immediately afterward they heard all the elegant grooming implements Merlin kept on the edge of the sink clattering to the tiled floor.

"It seems our Chinese visitor is awake," said Merlin, brushing a few sesame seeds from his vest. "Come, my friend. Let us put our heads together and consider how we can unfetch a *ying-long.*"

Wycca was awakened from a fitful sleep not by the heat, but by an urge more powerful than the urge to build her nest, more overwhelming than the instinct to protect her egg. She was overcome with the need to seek out and consume more chocolate, and being a wyvern, she would pursue that goal as single-mindedly as though chocolate were an unfettered spell she must destroy.

But as soon as she landed on the M.I.T. dome, Wycca could see unpromising activity on the roof of the New England Confectionary Company. Men in hard hats were swarming over its surface, some inspecting the exhaust vents and other structures, while others tacked heavy wire mesh over the vent Wycca had used to gain entry to the factory the day before. But even more discouraging, there was no mouthwatering aroma of chocolate cherry cordials wafting from the factory's smokestack. Even if she could find a new way in, Wycca was not sure she would find a reward inside. There were also two trucks parked at the loading dock, one a streamlined white van with darkened windows and the words NIPPON ROBOTICS printed on it in silvery blue, the other a battered gray truck with ominous tanks and hoses and a large cockroach on the roof. CREEPY CRAWLERS PEST CONTROL was painted on the side of the truck in red.

There were promising if faint smells issuing from Rosie's Bakery in Inman Square, but on closer inspection Wycca discovered it was too hot to run the large ovens, and the cupcakes and brownies had all been moved to refrigerated cases to keep them from melting. Wycca had to content herself with chocolate icing licked from discarded wrappers and cake boxes in the bakery's Dumpster—all the while kicking and hissing at an enraged terrier who had dashed out of a nearby yard to nip at her heels.

Mere traces of icing were not very satisfying. Wycca prowled along the alley that ran behind Cambridge Street, through the backyards of convenience stores and coffeehouses and restaurants. There were strong smells, the sour reek of ripe garbage and old beer, mingled with delicious smells of coffee brewing and meat slowly smoking, and from the vents of laundry rooms, the smell of clean towels drying in the dryer. Wycca sorted the smells carefully, but she did not smell—

Wait.

Was it—?

Could it—?

It *was.*

It was different, not melting and soft and gooey and sweet with cherry fondant filling. It was cold, its aroma more subtle, trapped in ice crystals, but there was no mistaking it.

It was chocolate.

The back door of Coneheads Ice Cream was open, and the screen door had been left on the latch. Carrie, the owner, and her two part-time employees were in the front of the shop, scooping up ice cream as fast as they could to serve a line of heatstruck customers that stretched out the front door and down the sidewalk.

A new batch of ice cream had been left in one of the big commercial ice-cream churns, ready to be packed into large round cardboard tubs. Carrie was a chocolate fanatic herself, and her chocolate flavors—Chocolate Insanity, Beyond Insanity, and a variation on Rocky Road called Geology Field Trip—had won prizes at food contests around New England. The churn was full of a new flavor Carrie had been perfecting for the upcoming Chocolate Challenge Food Festival. She had blended deep, dark, bittersweet chocolate ice cream with whole toasted Brazil nuts and chocolate-covered coffee beans. Carrie called it Toucan's Chocolate Addiction.

Wycca lowered her beak into the stainless-steel bowl and sampled the frozen chocolate. She drew her beak back in surprise, rolling the crunchy bits around in her beak with her black, muscular tongue. Deciding she liked this unfamiliar texture and new taste, she gave a greedy squeal and dipped her head back in.

Soon Wycca had climbed into the bowl of the churn, burrowing headfirst into the ice cream. Immersed in frozen chocolate, the wyvern began to eat, her purrs blending in with the loud hum of the large restaurant freezers.

When the rush of customers had died down Carrie remembered the abandoned batch of Toucan's Addiction. She hurried into the kitchen to get the ice cream packed and into the freezer. She found the stainless-steel bowl licked clean and a trail of strange footprints leading to a torn screen door.

Theodora paused inside the door of Traveler's Tales while her eyes adjusted to the dim interior. Through the gloom she could make out the familiar racks of new comics, the long bins of used comics in plastic sleeves, the tall spinning racks with sheets of collectible stickers, and the long, locked glass cases full of trading cards. All the light in the room seemed to come from the case that held the *Wizards & Wyverns* items: trading cards, pewter game pieces, temporary tattoos, magic disappearing and reappearing ink, and all the rest. At the back of the store a heavy velvet curtain, midnight blue and patterned with silver stars and planets, hung across the doorway to the back room where the Wyvernkeeper's Circle met.

The song playing on the boom box behind the counter stopped, and for a moment Theodora could hear dice being rolled in the back room, followed by a groan and a triumphant cackle as piles of tokens changed hands.

The next song started—by a band Milo liked called Said the Caterpillar—and the girl behind the counter looked up. She wore her hair, dyed a raven black, in dozens of tightly coiled knobs all over her head, like little snails. She had on fluorescent orange eye shadow and black lipstick, and along her collarbone was a tattoo of Egyptian hieroglyphics.

"Hey, Theodora. You've been scarce."

"Hey, Gina." Careful not to disturb the iguana who was napping on top of the cash register, Theodora hoisted her backpack onto the counter and took out her deck of *Wizards & Wyverns* cards, rubber-banded together, each in its own protective plastic sleeve. She spread them out on the counter in the usual array—wyvern cards in a row across the top, trait cards arranged below them. Gina leaned forward.

"The whole array." She nodded her approval. "So you finally got that last wyvern card."

Theodora nodded, handing the card with the wyvern and the imp to Gina. Her heart was beating really fast, and she could feel herself starting to turn red. But suddenly she grew very calm and heard her voice saying the words she had practiced so carefully in front of the bathroom mirror.

"Well, I'm not sure. It looks kind of funny, doesn't it? I wondered if it might be one of those fake cards from Hong Kong."

Gina turned up the lights and looked at the card with a magnifying glass. "Yeah, I see what you mean," she said, pushing it back toward Theodora. "Where did you get it?"

"It was the weirdest thing. It was stuck to my shoe in Central Square, all covered with gunk. We took it home and cleaned it off and let it dry." Theodora wrinkled her brow and looked up at Gina with the best puzzled look she could muster. "But I just don't know—should it count? I mean, it doesn't seem right to count it toward the Wyvernkeeper's Circle if it's not a regulation-issue card."

"Wait here." Gina slid off her stool, picked the card back up, and went toward the back of the shop. She pulled aside the curtain and said something that was too muffled to make out. The rattle of dice and tokens stopped, and voices were raised in impassioned discussion. After a minute or two Gina returned to the counter.

"It's an amazing card," Gina said, returning the card to its spot in the array on the counter. "But since it's not official, they feel it's not fair to offer you a full membership. But they said you could sit in on a Circle meeting, like a probationary member, with reduced privileges."

"Reduced? Reduced how, exactly?" Theodora asked.

"Well, basically, you can watch, but you can't play or vote or speak unless you're addressed directly. And you'd have to run out to get refreshments."

"I see." Theodora could feel her face flushing hot. She gathered up the cards and snapped the rubber band back around them. She dropped the deck in her backpack and tightened the drawstring. "So I'm not good enough to be a real member, but I'm good enough to be their indentured servant and wait on them hand and foot."

"Hey," said Gina, lowering her voice and putting on her older, wiser woman face. "Between you and me, your card is way cooler than all theirs put together. Go start your own club. Besides, you really don't want to hang out with them. Trust me."

But Theodora was already out the door and down the stairs.

Start her own club? "Yeah, me and who else?" she muttered as she stepped out onto the sidewalk. Even when Milo and Valerie were around, they weren't that interested in wyvern stuff. She could just see it: sitting all alone in her top-secret clubhouse, saying the secret password to herself, putting a splint on the broken wing of a wyvern puppet.

You just didn't get much more pathetic than that.

But by the time she reached her own street, she was fine-tuning a vivid fantasy that involved her walking into Traveler's Tales with a real, live wyvern on a leash.

"Of course you can pet her," she said under her breath, "once you've served your six-month probation and scored sixteen hundred on your wyvernkeeper aptitude test."

11

Wyvern's Milk

IT HAD TURNED into a steamy summer's day, and the air-conditioning of the Agassiz Arms had promptly refused to function. In Merlin's small apartment the heat was oppressive. Gideon was sprawled in a chair in the study, idly pouring Ignus from hand to hand as though he were a Slinky. Merlin was at the desk bent over his copy of *F.S.S.S.B IV,* tapping a fountain pen thoughtfully against his front teeth as he read. A single electric fan was stirring the warm air to and fro. Ouroboros was coiled around a glass of iced tea, sipping through two straws while he read the *Harvard Gazette.*

Gideon spoke. "Would it not be easier to summon the Chinaman who brought our repast in white boxes and bid him to take the *ying-long* back with him to China?"

Merlin looked up from *Fetching, Summoning, and Sundry Spells of Binding,* which he had open to the chapter on Unfetching.

"I am flattered you think me wizard enough to summon dinner from the far side of the globe, but I fear you have an exaggerated notion of my powers. I did summon the Chinaman, as you call him, but only from the Golden Panda restaurant in Harvard Square. He sped here not on the wings of a spell, but on a motorized menace called a moped."

Gideon let Ignus flow from his hand back onto the mantelpiece. "What does the book say about unfetching Chinese dragons?"

"Well, water dragons can be safely deposited in running water so long as it has an outlet to the sea—you don't want to drop them down a well or into a lake, for they will just make trouble. Alas, our *ying-long* is rather too conspicuous to smuggle down to the banks of the Charles River. In the meantime, I am afraid he will eat us out of house and home."

The two wizards had puzzled about what to feed their accidental houseguest. At last, at the suggestion of Ouroboros, they had filled the bathtub with a porridge of rice and jasmine tea, and the *ying-long* had happily fed from the makeshift trough. The Chinese dragon also seemed to like microwave popcorn (Merlin theorized that the explosive popping was not unlike the sound of Chinese firecrackers). For now the *ying-long* was sleeping off breakfast, but they were out of popcorn and dangerously low on rice and tea, and there was a ring of porridge in the tub that would have to be removed, Merlin had remarked darkly, "with a jackhammer."

Exhausted from the sultry heat and from racking their brains, the two wizards fell silent, only to be roused by a sudden noisy rattle of air in the drinking straws as Ouroboros ran out of iced tea.

"I believe I have thought of a solution," said the snake. "Merlin, have you any garments that might pass as Chinese?"

Merlin thought a moment. "With a little translation from the Japanese," he said, "I played the title role in *The Mikado* this past fall. My costume was a set of rather splendid robes. If I can find them, it wouldn't take much to alter them. And we can always see what a little Wizard's Latin will do for Gideon."

"Ouroboros, what plot have you hatched?" asked Gideon warily.

"Listen," said the wise old snake, "and I will tell you."

Mikko and Theodora were in the backyard, their lawn chairs strategically placed in the path of the sprinkler.

They were wearing bathing suits and eating fruitsicles. Theodora was reading a battered old copy of *Harriet the Spy*, keeping the book dry under the plastic splatter shield Mikko used to protect her cookbooks in the kitchen.

When Theodora finished her fruitsicle, Mikko reached into a small cooler beside her chair and handed her a new one.

"That's the last raspberry," she said. "There's one more pineapple and the rest are coconut."

Theodora wrinkled her nose. *Coconut.*

"Mikko?"

"Mmm?"

"Can we sleep out here tonight?"

"Well, maybe just a game of Moonlight Ping-Pong before lights-out."

Andy Oglethorpe had invented Moonlight Ping-Pong when he was a graduate student, and the Oglethorpes still owned a Ping-Pong table with the lines marked out in reflective tape and a supply of paddles and Ping-Pong balls sprayed with fluorescent paint.

For the first time since they had found the wyvern card in the street, things felt almost normal. The awful knot in her chest Theodora always felt when she and Mikko had a fight was almost completely undone. The heat wave had helped, giving them a common enemy. Theodora bit off a chunk of her raspberry fruitsicle and thought that it was good to have Mikko around. It made up for Milo and Valerie deserting her almost until school started up again. It nearly even made up for her dad leaving her behind like she was still ten or something, while he went off into the jungle to make important discoveries.

Just then Theodora's brain decided it would be a good moment to replay a memory of her mom, laughing and chasing Theodora around the backyard with the hose on a hot August afternoon. Theodora jerked in her lawn chair, so that Mikko slid her sunglasses down on her nose to see her better.

"You okay?"

"Uh-huh. It was just a bee."

Her brain had a way of doing that, Theodora thought to herself: reminding her that, no matter how good life got with Mikko around, things could never be the same.

During heat waves Mikko's cat usually sought relief in the cellar or on the cool tiled floor of the Oglethorpes' bathroom. But today Frankie was hunched unhappily on the end of Mikko's bed, his exit blocked by the card that lay on the dresser. That morning Mikko had moved the wyvern card from the kitchen to her bedroom for safekeeping, and Frankie had refused to venture past it, even though it stood between him and all his comforts: food, water, litter box, and Mikko.

Every now and then a faint breeze from the window would lift one edge of the card, and the cat would arch his back and hiss. He was old and—as Mikko put it in the fondest possible way—"a cat of very little brain." But like most animals, he knew something otherworldly when he ran across it, and he did not like the wyvern card, not even a little bit. It was old and powerful, and it had the unmistakable whiff of magic about it.

Frankie flattened himself against the bedspread and moaned miserably.

Presenting themselves as Mr. Lambton and Ms. Worm, Kobold and Febrys had worked their way down the alphabetical list, visiting the establishments of Ebeneezer Abernathy, Antiquarian Bookseller; Cosmo Constantinopolous, Books & Manuscripts; and Mortimer Featherstone, Fine & Rare Books—all to no avail.

They were on their way to the next bookstore when they had to stop at the drugstore at the foot of Charles Street to buy more corn pads for Febrys's feet.

"Not all human women wear these shoes," the demon said sulkily as they walked down the aisle of foot-care products. "Some of them wear Birkenstocks and Nikes." Febrys had seen ads for them on the large-screen TV in the penthouse.

"Your feet are cloven," Kobold said. "They would hurt no matter what human shoes you put on them."

"I do not think so," said Febrys. "I think that—*ribbit!*"

Febrys clapped a hand over her mouth. The stock boy in a blue apron who was putting prices on cans of athlete's-foot spray turned and gawked.

Kobold took the demon by the arm and walked quickly to the checkout.

The checkout clerk looked suspiciously at them over her half-moon glasses.

"Is she okay? Ma'am, do you feel all right?"

Febrys opened her mouth and promptly turned a froggy croak into a hacking cough.

"Poor dear! You sound terrible." The clerk took a few cough drops from a display and dropped them into the plastic bag with the corn pads. "Those are on the house."

"Thank you," said Kobold, reaching for the bag.

Febrys was now gagging and wheezing so loudly that other customers were backing away from them. Drawing a long, gasping breath, her eyes almost popping out of her head, the demon hacked a small, green glob onto the checkout belt.

"Eeeeew!" Eight customers waiting in line recoiled in unison.

Then the small, green glob opened its eyes and began to stretch its legs.

"Ribbit," it said.

"It's a *frog!*" someone exclaimed.

"Ribbit," said the frog, hopping over to a display of lip balm.

"Hey, that's pretty funny," said the man in line behind them.

The checkout clerk suddenly pointed a finger at Kobold.

"I know you! You're that magician, the one who's got the show at the Emerson Majestic." She turned to Febrys. "And you must be the girl he saws in thirds."

Kobold made a deep, dramatic bow. "You may keep the frog as a souvenir."

Outside on the sidewalk the wizard turned to his demon.

"Do not utter the words *I think* in my presence."

Febrys rubbed her throat and shook her head. Even with their green contact lenses, her demon eyes had a new, sullen gleam to them.

Wycca's binge at the confectionery factory the day before had stretched her already-elastic stomach. Now the ice cream she had gorged on made her look as though she had swallowed a beach ball. The mixture of chocolate and coffee beans had left her with plenty of mischief to burn off, but her enormous belly left her too heavy to hide in one of the tunnels that ran beneath Boston Harbor.

Wycca flew back to the nest, losing a few scales as she squeezed in at the window. She tried in vain to settle her own round form on top of her egg. It was like trying to balance a watermelon on top of a grape. At last she had to settle for curling up around her egg, with one wing draped protectively over it.

She had just drifted off when a faint sound jerked her awake again. It was barely audible but unmistakable: the sound of a tiny wyvern's beak tapping on the inside of an eggshell. Her egg was ready to hatch.

As the tiny beak emerged and widened the opening, Wycca gently used her own beak to clear away shell fragments but otherwise let her offspring struggle free on its own, encouraging it with soothing purrs in response to its plaintive *wroa-wroa.* At last the baby wyvern emerged, damp and blind. Its wings were crumpled against its back, and its outsized head was too heavy for it to hold upright. Its large eyes were closed, their transparent lids webbed with tiny, pink blood vessels. It was really a very homely creature, one only a mother could love. And Wycca did, instantly and fiercely, with her whole wyvern being.

She removed all the shards of eggshell from the nest and then gave her baby a thorough bath, from the tip of its rubbery beak (it would not toughen for a week or so) to the stub of its short, pointed tail. Using her beak, she nudged it closer so that it was nuzzled close to her belly.

At last it found one of a pair of teats and latched on, clinging to her with its small, sharp talons. It is hard for a creature with a bill to nurse, but it is a feat managed by baby platypuses and some of the smaller dragons.

And so Wycca unwittingly introduced her hatchling to chocolate, in the form of wyvern's milk, strongly flavored with Toucan's Chocolate Addiction.

12

A Wizard's Trump

BLUE-AND-WHITE-striped tents had been pitched along the bank of the Charles River, and from their shade vendors were hawking Chinese refreshments and traditional crafts. At one booth kids were having their faces painted to resemble the Monkey King and other characters from the Peking Opera. Nearby on a makeshift stage students from a local martial-arts school were doing a kung fu demonstration. A small crowd had gathered to watch, and a few dozen people were strolling around eating grilled chicken from bamboo skewers. But everyone else at the Dragon Boat

Festival was jammed along the five-hundred-meter course, jostling for position on the riverbank and on the footbridge from which to watch the start of the Boston Dragon Boat Races.

A dozen sleek, brightly painted teak boats, their prows carved and gilded to resemble dragons, had assembled down by the Cambridge Boat House for the start of the race. Whereas a regular boat with a crew of eight would have a coxswain to urge the rowers on and help steer the course, the dragon boats had crews of eighteen: eight pairs of paddlers, seated side by side; a steerperson at the rudder; and a drummer perched in the stern to set the pace. There were dragon-boat crews sporting T-shirts of local colleges and high-tech companies and Boston radio stations, but other crews had come all the way from Singapore and Australia. Some of the rowers called back and forth to one another in friendly rivalry.

A late entry into the race was hugging the shore not far from the starting line, riding perilously low in the water. It was a very old boat, and a member of the Harvard class of 1936 with a good memory might have recognized it as the scull that had won the Regatta that year, with a young Iain M. O'Shea as its captain. It seemed to have a crew of two: one portly older man wearing voluminous red and gold robes, with a vaguely Mandarin-style cap, and a younger, thinner man in a set of black academic robes with a gold dragon motif stenciled around the sleeves and hem. What seemed to be a pile of old life preservers under a green tarpaulin was making strange whuffling noises. From time to time the men would bend over the pile and shush it.

"We do not blend in, Merlin," said Gideon as the crew from the Smith College boat craned their necks to get a better look at them.

Merlin was busy tucking the tarpaulin more tightly around the *ying-long.* "I'm afraid we are a little conspicuous. But I wager the real boat crews will assume we are hired entertainment for the kiddies, as long as we stay out of their way."

At the starting line a trumpeter sounded a blast on a strange-looking long horn, and the race was on: the paddlers paddled furiously in time to the drummed beat; spectators leaned over the railings of the bridges across the Charles, cheering on their teams and blowing on smaller horns. The sleek, dragon-nosed boats sped away down the water.

Bringing up the rear, the scull with Merlin and Gideon came limping after, and as it passed under the first of the bridges, there was a loud splash. When the boat emerged on the other side of the bridge, it was riding considerably higher in the water, and both Merlin and Gideon were soaked to the skin.

Gideon peered over the side. "Farewell, *ying-long.* Godspeed you to your home."

"Let's hope it *is* farewell," said Merlin. "Let's hope he finds his way to the sea and not into a display tank at the New England Aquarium. Or worse, back to our doorstep in search of more porridge and popcorn."

The shop of Giles and Moira Hatch, Booksellers, was located in the Italian neighborhood of Boston's North End, in a third-floor loft in a former shoe factory. Mikko and Theodora passed the large *salumeria* on the corner, breathing in the spicy, garlicky smells of sausages and olives, and the Tower of Pisa coffeehouse, with its nattily dressed old men sitting around reading Italian newspapers, and its plastic replicas of spumoni ice cream and cannoli arranged in the front window.

To get to the third floor, Theodora and Mikko had to ride in the building's ancient elevator, which had padded maroon leather doors with porthole windows set in them and a corroded dial with a quavering arrow that pointed out the brass numbers of the passing floors as they ascended.

The Hatches had the third floor all to themselves, and they had made the hallway more presentable with some worn but still beautiful old rugs and a couple of unkillable rubber trees that didn't mind the lack of light. A sign with an arrow pointing left directed them, THIS WAY TO THE BOOKS.

Theodora was expecting an old couple: a woman with

her hair up in a bun and half glasses on a chain around her neck, and a man in a jacket with leather patches on the elbows, smoking a pipe. So the Hatches were a big surprise: much younger than she had pictured them, a little older than her dad, maybe (of course, that was still old, but it wasn't *decrepit*). Giles Hatch was wearing a polo shirt and shorts and old tennis shoes splattered with about six different colors of house paint. You could see one of his toes through the worn canvas. Moira's hair was prematurely silver, cut so short it was almost a crew cut, and she was wearing a flowing pantsuit of paprika-colored gauze and a necklace of chunky African beads.

They greeted Mikko with kisses and exclamations of delight, and soon they were all seated in surprisingly comfortable lumpy armchairs, drinking iced tea.

Moira and Mikko had to finish exchanging news about people they had both known when they worked together in an auction house, but at last Moira shot Giles a sideways glance and laughed.

"All right," she said. "You'd better get that mysterious card out, or poor Giles might explode."

They went over to a plain wooden worktable, and Mikko opened her purse and took out the small manila envelope that had the card in it, safely sandwiched between layers of tissue and cardboard. She handed the card to Giles, who placed it on the table and set some small glass weights on the corners of the card to hold it down. Then he swiveled into position a magnifying lamp—much like the one Dr. Naga used to paint by—and switched it on.

Giles bent closely over the card for several minutes, muttering softly, "Uh-hum. Uh-hum. Right." He straightened up. "Moira, see what you think."

Moira peered through the lens at the card. "Mikko, you say you cleaned it?"

"Yes. Just first aid, to get off the worst of the grime and dirt. Whenever I wasn't sure whether I was taking off gunk or paint, I left it alone."

Moira nodded approvingly. "You did very well. I think the damaged spots are probably original wear and not anything you removed by mistake." She lifted the small weights from the corners and carefully turned the card over to study the pattern on the reverse. Then she turned it right side up and replaced the weights.

"Well, what you've got—and chime in here, Giles, if I've got it wrong—is a thirteenth-century tarot card in the Italian style. I say *style* because there are one or two things about it that make me think the artist was working outside Italy, perhaps outside the continent entirely."

Giles nodded his head in agreement. "Yes. Trained in Italy but working, I'd guess, at the court of a noble patron in the British Isles."

Theodora gulped and stared at the card, wondering how they could tell all that.

"But the most striking thing about it," Moira continued, "is that it is extremely early for a tarot card. Most of the famous decks passed down in the great noble families of Italy date from the mid-1400s. There are some very early tarot cards from the 1320s in Germany. But I would put the date of this deck even earlier, around 1260, give or take thirty years on either side." Moira smiled at Theodora. "That makes this card very special. Not as special as if you could prove where it came from, or if you had some of the rest of the deck, but still special."

"Special indeed," said a man's voice.

They all jumped. No one had noticed a couple enter the bookshop. They had managed to approach within feet of the table without making a noise. The man was young, but his stern expression—handsome features carved into a permanent frown—made him seem much older. He wore a dark gray suit and carried a walking stick topped with a large piece of polished quartz, like a small crystal ball. His companion was dressed in a fashionable suit of soft gray silk, but something about her appearance, perhaps the unearthly green of her eyes, made her appear downright creepy. When she smiled at them she had small, even, rounded teeth, like a doll's. The sight of them made Theodora shudder.

Mikko calmly picked up the tarot card and slipped it into her bag, which she held casually in an expert anti-pickpocket grip.

"Yes," she said calmly. "So special, we will be taking it straight to the medieval art experts at the Museum of Fine Arts."

The man blinked, then reached into the inner pocket of his jacket and removed a thin silver case. He drew out a business card and handed it to Giles. Giles looked at it and passed it to Moira, who passed it to Mikko. Theodora leaned over Mikko's shoulder and read:

KONRAD LAMBTON

Nothing more: no company address, no phone number, no fax or E-mail. Just KONRAD LAMBTON, printed in raised black type on a heavy, ivory card.

"May I present my associate, Ms. Worm?" said Mr. Lambton. Ms. Worm suddenly tottered a few steps toward them, as though she had been pushed, but quickly regained her balance and smiled another eerie doll's smile.

Moira folded her arms across her chest and tilted her head to one side. "What kind of business are you and your associate in, Mr. Lambton? I don't think I've seen you on the rare book show circuit."

"No?" Mr. Lambton ran a gloved finger along the spines of the leather-bound books on the nearest shelf. "Well, I am not surprised. I am a private collector living abroad."

"What exactly do you collect?" asked Giles.

"Medieval manuscripts," said Mr. Lambton. "Especially those with a connection to the occult. I am particularly keen to acquire tarot cards like the remarkable example Miss Kolodney has in her handbag."

Mikko was unruffled. "I would like to know how you know my last name," she said. "I don't recall introducing myself."

Mr. Lambton only smiled an inscrutable smile. "Whatever the museum offers you for the card, I will double the offer."

Mikko and Moira didn't react, but Giles opened his mouth and closed it wordlessly, giving his wife a desperate glance. She ignored him.

"Considering your card doesn't have anything on it but your name, how would we even get in touch with you?" Mikko said. She still had the veteran subway rider's iron grip on her bag. Theodora noticed that Mr. Lambton looked at the handbag—a vintage 1950s embroidered bag with a metal chain—hungrily, but also fearfully. She wondered why.

"Oh, don't worry. I will get in touch with you," said Mr. Lambton. "Come, Ms. Worm. We will show ourselves out. Mr. and Mrs. Hatch. Miss Kolodney. Miss Oglethorpe. It has been our pleasure." He bowed deeply, extending his walking stick with a flourish, and they turned and left.

Moira Hatch let out a long breath and sat down. Giles Hatch sat down beside her and groaned.

"Why are the richest buyers also the crookedest?"

"You think he was crooked?" Mikko asked.

They both nodded their heads vigorously.

"That tripe he told us about being a private collector living abroad," said Giles. "Most of the private collectors I know living abroad are boards of Japanese corporations or eccentric Dutch millionaires in running shoes. He's the kind of private collector you'd invent if you'd never met one. The *gloves.* The *walking* stick, for Pete's sake."

Moira was shaking her head thoughtfully. "Still . . ."

Mikko looked at her. "Still what?"

"I think he was crooked—no doubt about it—how else could he have found out all our names unless he was up to some con game? But I'd bet anything he knows something about that card. Before you slipped it into your bag, I saw him looking at it. Greedily."

Theodora hadn't said much, but she suddenly spoke up. "It was almost as though he was afraid to touch it."

All three adults just turned and looked at her. Then Mikko suddenly grabbed her handbag and opened it. The wyvern and imp card slid out onto the table, and the late-afternoon light from the loft windows struck the brilliant paint and set the colors aglow.

"I just wanted to make sure it was still there and

hadn't turned into purse lint or fairy dust," she said a little sheepishly.

Moira wrapped the card up again, this time in a sandwich of acid-free tissue and special archivists' book-mending cardboard. Once it had been returned to the safety of Mikko's handbag, Giles declared it was just late enough for an early dinner at Old Angelo's around the corner.

"And then a movie?" said Theodora hopefully.

"An air-conditioned movie," said Moira emphatically.

13

Make a Wish

FEBRYS WAS IN the bathroom of the penthouse apartment, soaking her feet in the bathtub. *Bathtub* did not really do it justice. The size of a small swimming pool, the pink marble tub had three steps leading up to it and three steps leading down into the swirling, heated water, which issued from gold-plated faucets in the form of dolphins all around the edge of the circular basin. The water frothed and foamed around the demon's bruised and battered feet. She sighed with pleasure.

Out in the apartment the doorbell sounded, and Kobold went to answer it. A deliveryman in a brown uniform handed him an electronic clipboard. Kobold took the stylus and wrote *Konrad Lambton.* He handed the clipboard back, took the small parcel handed to him, and closed the door.

Kobold carried the parcel to the glass-and-chrome dining room table and set it down. "Undo," he commanded, and the parcel promptly began to unwrap itself, the tape unpeeling and the paper unfolding to reveal a layer of bubble wrap underneath.

"All the way," Kobold added peevishly.

The bubble wrap fell away to reveal a book. It had once been bound in red leather, its cover set with moonstones and serpentines that would have winked like animal eyes. This copy had been assembled from the remains of at least three tattered copies, much worried by wyverns. The surviving pages, skillfully mended, had been bound in plain green cloth.

Kobold picked up the book and opened it to the first page.

The Book of the New Adept

or,

Secrets of the Wizard's

Guild Revealed

Of course, since the printing press had not yet been invented in the year 900, these words were in Latin, handwritten in black Gothic letters.

There was a note enclosed with the book, from Prunella Snipes, Bookseller.

My dear Mr. Lambton,

My friend and colleague, Mr. Ebeneezer Abernathy, has informed me that you are anxious to acquire a copy of this book. As it happens, I had just completed a restoration of this badly damaged copy. Note the remaining imperfections. If it is acceptable to you in this condition, please reply to the address above. The terms of payment are cash, thirty days.

Yours sincerely,
P. Snipes

Kobold set the book and the note down on the table. With the forbidden spell contained in the book, he could summon a shadow wyvern to capture Gideon's familiar and ultimately destroy his rival. But with the wyvern card he had seen yesterday, in the possession of the young woman and girl, he could cast an even darker spell—one that would enhance his powers and give him a more satisfying revenge over his half brother.

But the card's powers were such that it could not be taken by spell or by force. It would have to be handed over willingly. That seemed unlikely, unless . . .

Unless.

In the bathroom Febrys was ignoring her master's summons, giving her two long demon toes a last wiggle, when the water abruptly stopped flowing from the golden spigots. With a whimper, Febrys scrambled out of the tub. If he was sufficiently annoyed, Kobold might replace the water coming out of the jets with something unpleasant, like fetid gray slime or boiling mud that smelled of rotten eggs.

She appeared in the living room doorway. "Yes, my master."

"I have a task for you, but first you must take a new form."

Febrys hissed in dismay. The discomforts of human woman shoes aside, she liked this form better than any other she had been called on to assume, and far better than her true demon appearance. But she was bound to obey Kobold.

The wizard picked up the telephone and dialed a number.

"Unified Parcel Systems? I would like to arrange for a package to be picked up at my apartment." There was a pause as the person on the other end spoke, then Kobold smiled, with a sidelong glance at his demon.

"Yes, it's ready to be picked up now."

At Merlin's apartment at the Agassiz Arms, things were almost back to normal. All the fetching apparatus had been put away, and elbow grease and a little magic had removed most traces of the *ying-long.* Gideon used a simple spell to animate a box of steel-wool pads and set them to work on the porridge ring in the bathtub. It was satisfying to hear them scrubbing away; it had been days since he had stretched his spell-casting muscles, and the technological wonders that confronted him at every turn had left him feeling that his wizardly powers were dull indeed.

He sorely missed his early morning training sessions with Wycca. He had been in the habit of taking her out in the gray of the dawn, when the meadow was still cloaked in mist. Gideon would take with him a sack of small spells and lob them into the air for Wycca to retrieve. It was good exercise for them both, and for the space of an hour it kept the wyvern from her mischief and kept his own mind from thoughts of Gwynlyn.

He left the Brillo pads scrubbing away and went into the living room.

"Ouroboros."

The snake raised his heads from the back of the sofa, where he had been napping. "Yesss?"

"Can you consult your forward memory and tell me whether Wycca's egg has hatched?"

Ouroboros closed his eyes for a moment, then opened them. "I'm sorry, Gideon. Nothing." While the snake's memory did function as well forward as it did backward, it was not very reliable for events in the near future and recent past. His memory was farsighted; it was much sharper when it came to events decades and even centuries off in either direction.

"I hoped perhaps here it might be a little clearer." Gideon counted days and nights in his head. It was now the fifth day since they had followed the wyvern through the bolt-hole. She had no doubt laid her egg as soon as she had found a safe nesting spot. Given the summer heat and rapid dragonling development, it had probably hatched already. So Gideon now had two wyverns to find before Kobold did.

He retrieved his satchel from the coat closet and got out his velvet-wrapped deck of wyvern cards. Now, as he began to lay the cards out in a T on the coffee table, his hand froze. With shaking fingers, he rapidly fanned through the deck, then again in disbelief.

The Talent card for the wyvern was gone. Gideon fell back against the sofa cushions with a hoarse cry that brought Merlin from the bedroom at a trot.

"Good heavens! Gideon, whatever is it?"

The younger wizard's face was ashen, and his mouth had gone so dry with fear that he had to lick his lips before he could speak, and then only in jumbled phrases.

"A card . . . A card is gone from my deck. The worst possible card. A trump . . . a wyvern trump . . ."

Merlin sank down onto the sofa beside him. "Oh, dear."

The younger wizard was now almost panic-stricken. What Gideon and Merlin both knew was that Kobold could use the trump to trap him forever in an endless loop of his most painful memories—a horrible, never-ending mental torture from which a death by Turning would be a blessing. And that would only be the beginning.

Gideon clenched his fists. "I know exactly when it happened! When I came through the bolt-hole, into the nightstick—"

"Nightclub," corrected Merlin.

"—into the nightclub. I had to retrieve the contents of my pockets from a pickpocket. The deck was only loosely wrapped. I am sure the card fell out then." Gideon leaped up from the sofa. "We must find it."

"Gideon, I am afraid it is almost impossible. There are great yellow noisy machines that go up and down the streets of Cambridge once a week, sucking up the litter in the gutters. If your trump card hasn't been spit out in a landfill, it has probably long since been washed down a storm drain into the city sewers."

Merlin's face was furrowed in concentration. "Now, we ordinarily could use your deck to ask a question, but since it isn't complete, that won't work. And we can't use my deck. It's on loan to a museum in Italy. I was always rusty in my card skills, anyway."

He got up and went to the coat closet and began rummaging on a top shelf. "Risk, Monopoly, Clue . . . ah. Got it."

From under a pile of board games, Merlin drew a slender carved box from which he removed and unfolded a Ouija fortune-telling board, except this one obviously had not come from the game aisle of a Toys "R" Us. Instead of printed paper pasted to cardboard, this set gleamed with rare woods and winked with inset mirrors, pearls, and rubies.

The older wizard cleared a space on the coffee table and set out the board and the planchette, a triangular piece of inlaid wood on small wheels.

"Mass-produced sets are cheap cardboard, of course, not rosewood set with ivory. But this is a custom set from India, made in Pondicherry around 1920. It belonged to the son of a maharaja who just happened to be my lab partner in chemistry when I was at Harvard. He gave it to me in exchange for some tutoring. Of course, if you don't know how to ask the oracle properly, it's nothing more than a parlor game, but in the hands of a professional it's quite a useful little gadget."

He instructed Gideon to place his fingertips lightly on one side of the planchette and rested his own on the other. Merlin said a few quick phrases in Wizard's English, "just to calibrate the settings," then he cleared his throat and intoned: "Oh, Great Oracle, tell us the name of the person who possesses the lost wyvern trump of your faithful servant Gideon."

The planchette began to move lightly beneath their fingers, sliding from the center of the board over to the right and stopping at the letter T. It paused for a moment, then it was on the move again, wavering between G and I before coming to rest on the letter H.

So it went, letter after letter, and after the first dozen their fingers began to cramp up and their shoulders to ache. But at last the planchette was still.

Merlin wiggled his numb fingers. "That seems to be all for today. I make that out to spell *Theodora Oglethorpe.* Did you get the same?"

Gideon nodded, but he was staring down at the inlaid board, with its jeweled YES and NO. "Can the oracle tell us where Wycca is?"

Merlin drew himself up as though offended by the suggestion. "If it could, do you really think I would have made you wait five days and put you through a Fetching? Alas, the powers of the Ouija do not extend to creatures of magic, especially those that do not care to be found—such as a wyvern with a hatchling. Wycca's camouflage is too good, I'm afraid. But don't look so downcast, my friend. There's a very good chance our Miss Oglethorpe is in the Cambridge phone book."

Theodora *did* have the wyvern trump, not the laser-printed copy, but the original that Moira Hatch had wrapped so carefully in a sandwich of acid-free tissue and special bookbinder's board. Once a week Mikko called her best friend in Rochester, New York, and could be counted on to stay in her room for an hour. Once she had heard Mikko pick up the phone and start to dial, Theodora crept over to where Mikko's purse hung from the back of a chair and silently lifted out the card.

On the way home from the movie, Mikko had explained to Theodora that she had to decide on her own what to do about the card, knowing everything she did now. Mikko wasn't her guardian and she wasn't going to force a decision on her. If Theodora came to her own conclusion that it was the right thing to do, they would call the museum in the morning and arrange to deliver the card to the right curator. In the meantime, they would leave it wrapped up in Mikko's purse for safekeeping.

As she unwrapped it, Theodora told herself she was only going to look at it, just hold it for a minute, then put it right back. But once she had it in her hands, the inky blacks and glowing scarlets and rich purples seemed to make the image leap right off the card, and she felt a strange feeling come over her, an electric tingling through her fingers, up her arm, and into her brain. Distant sounds of the traffic on the street came to her muffled and distorted, as though she were underwater. When she thought about it later it seemed to her that she never *decided* to do anything that followed, but as she performed each action, no matter how childish or silly, it seemed perfectly natural, and not silly at all. It was as if the card itself was telling her what to do (which, while it wasn't *technically* true, was more or less what was happening).

So, when Merlin posed the question to the Ouija board, the wyvern trump was quite literally in Theodora's hands. She wasn't sure why she needed to take it out, except she couldn't seem to get out of her head the expression on Mr. Lambton's face when he had looked at the tarot card—as if it were a cross between a winning lottery ticket worth thirty million dollars and a radio-active time bomb.

Theodora got out her *Wizards & Wyverns* deck and placed her seven Wyvern suit cards in a row on the foot of her bed: Red, Green, Purple, Black, White, Silver, and Gold. Beneath each wyvern card she placed the appropriate Power, Frailty, and Wand cards, placing her copy of the magical card where the Black Wyvern's Power card should be.

She decided she needed a ceremony. There wasn't any incense in the house, so she went and got the Easter Island head ashtray someone had given her father as a joke, some dried rosemary leaves, and matches from the kitchen. Then she draped a sheer purple scarf over her bedside lamp, bathing the walls in amethyst light and shadow. An anti-stress cassette that her father had used to quit smoking provided the right combination of flute music and a gentle waterfall.

Finally Theodora dressed herself in a vest Aunt Jane had sent from China, silk brocade in a pattern of dragons, along with some baggy black leggings and a pair of Turkish slippers her grandmother had given her. To complete the look, she fished through her jewelry box, passing over an owl pendant in favor of an old brooch of her mother's, an abstract swirl that resembled a crouching dragon. She had never worn it to school because it looked too goofy, but for a secret ceremony it was perfect.

Theodora placed a generous handful of rosemary in the Easter Island head and struck a match. Sweet pine-scented smoke began to curl from the head's eyes in a suitably spooky way. Theodora set the ashtray on her dresser, coughing a little.

Facing the array of cards, she picked up Gideon's wyvern trump and held it high over her head.

"Send me a wyvern," she said, surprised at how confident her voice sounded. Part of her mind couldn't believe she was doing this, but it wasn't the part that seemed to be in control right at the moment.

"Send me a *wyvern,*" she said again, her voice clear and steady as though she summoned up mythical creatures every day a half hour before lunch. She calmly thought to herself that it didn't need to be a big wyvern; it should be small enough so that she could hide it from Mikko. She heard herself saying as much out loud, in a language she didn't recognize.

Startled, she looked down at the card in her hand. A pale light was coming from it and spreading up through her fingers, as though she were holding a handful of fireflies. She let the words flow out of her mouth. She had only taken Spanish in school and had no way of knowing she was speaking a peculiar dialect of medieval Latin.

Then the words stopped, the light from the card faded, and Theodora could feel her fingers tingling as the magic left them.

Suddenly she coughed and looked up. The room was growing hazy with smoke; she'd used a little too much rosemary. Finding herself still holding the card, she placed it in the empty spot in the array on her bedspread and touched her mother's brooch, feeling she should say something. Not *amen* or *abracadabra,* but something. But the card was now silent.

"Theodora Oglethorpe!"

Theodora whirled around to see Mikko in the doorway, cordless phone still in one hand. In all the years she had lived with them, Theodora had never seen Mikko look so angry.

In a single, seamless movement Mikko stepped into

the room, snatched up the Easter Island ashtray, and disappeared with it down the hall. Theodora heard the toilet flush.

Mikko reappeared and snatched the scarf from the bedside lamp. There was a dark circle in the center where the heat of the lamp had begun to scorch the fabric. Mikko sat down on the bed, shaking her head.

"Dodo, this is really, really serious. You could have started a fire. If the rosemary didn't start one, that flimsy scarf over the hot lightbulb was sure to. What am I going to do with you? Your father isn't coming home for weeks yet, and if you won't listen to me, I'll have to send you to your Uncle Hosmer for the rest of the summer."

Theodora went pale. Uncle Hosmer and Aunt Prue were really her great-great-uncle and great-great-aunt. They were about a million years old, and nothing in their tiny town house had changed since about 1965. They had never had any children of their own, so Aunt Prue's idea of a good time meant taking her to a sad, tacky village where they reenacted life in colonial America, and afterward they would go back to the tidy, silent town house and put on ruffled aprons and make elderberry jelly. They had done this on every visit since Theodora was five.

Mikko spotted the real tarot card among the array of cards laid out on the bed. She picked it up and looked at it disbelievingly for a long time. When she looked up at Theodora again, her eyes were red and her mouth was set in a thin line. "As for you helping yourself to something in my purse, your father will have to deal with that."

Tears stung Theodora's eyes. She was trying to think of something, anything, to say when they heard the front gate squeak. From the bedroom window they could see a brown delivery truck parked at the curb and a brown-uniformed driver making his way up the drive, wheeling a large cardboard box on a dolly.

Mikko got to her feet, the wyvern trump in one hand. "I'm going to go get that," she said. "When I get back I want all this put away."

She went to answer the door.

14

Demonizing Mikko

After Mikko left the room Theodora stood for a long moment, as though she had been turned to stone.

Suddenly she sprang into furious action. She peeled off her costume, wadded it into a big ball, and thrust it deep into the back of her closet. Next she swept her *Wizards & Wyverns* cards from the bedspread into a shoe box. From her closet she took an even bigger box and swept her entire shrine of wyvernalia into it: the Game-Bot cartridges, holographic tattoos, limited-edition sticker books and trading tokens, pewter figurines, everything. In a growing frenzy she yanked the papier-mâché wyvern down from the ceiling over her bed, punching and tearing and stomping it into a twisted pile of paper and sticks.

As she ripped her *Wizards & Wyverns* posters from the walls and tore them to confetti, she was sobbing with fury at herself. How could she have been such an idiot? Mikko would never trust her again. Theodora wouldn't be surprised if she quit when Theodora's dad got back. And Theodora wouldn't blame her much if she did.

When she finally stopped, flushed and panting in the middle of the floor, there wasn't a sign of *Wizards & Wyverns* left anywhere in her bedroom. After she had caught her breath, Theodora tugged the bedsheets smooth and pulled the quilt up over them. From under her bed she pulled a plastic laundry basket full of her old stuffed animals. She dusted off the patchwork dragon with sequin scales and a red felt tongue that had belonged to her mother, and returned it to a place of honor on her pillow.

It dawned on her that Mikko had been gone a long time. Opening the bedroom door, she poked her head out into the hallway. There was silence from the direction of the kitchen: no radio turned to the Brazilian music hour on WERS, no tropical pop songs blending with the sound of rhythmic chopping.

Theodora headed down the hallway and stopped

when she passed the living room. Mikko was stretched out, her bare feet propped up on one arm of the sofa. There were about a dozen little bottles of nail polish scattered across the coffee table, and Mikko's toes had been painted a rainbow of colors: mango, chartreuse, banana, fuchsia, chrome, grape, and navy.

What on earth was going on? Mikko always relaxed in her own room, only rarely joining the Oglethorpes in the living room to watch a movie. In the four years she had worked for them, Theodora had never, *never* seen Mikko put her feet up on the furniture. But even more amazing was the mess: there were drips and drizzles of nail polish all over the carpet and on the sofa cushions and a little pool of grape polish on the coffee table.

Theodora must have gasped, because Mikko raised herself on one elbow and turned around to look at her.

"Theodora, darling. How do you like my toes? Aren't they pretty?" She wiggled them appreciatively.

"Mikko, there's polish everywhere! Shouldn't we clean it up?"

Mikko glanced around and blinked. "I suppose."

Theodora folded her arms across her chest. "And it's almost two o'clock. When are we going to eat lunch?"

Now Mikko looked worried. "Lunch? You mean cooking it? Yes, I suppose I really should do something about that." She got to her feet, stepping in a little pool of chrome polish, and proceeded to make a silver trail of toe prints across the living room to the kitchen.

Theodora screwed the tops back on all the bottles of polish and dabbed at the spills as best she could with handfuls of tissues. As she blotted up the worst of the damage, her mind was racing. Maybe Mikko had gotten so angry, she'd temporarily gone insane. Or maybe she was just high on nail polish fumes. But what had possessed her to paint her toenails in the first place? Theodora would have thought she was drunk, only there wasn't any booze in the Oglethorpe household besides some Chinese cooking sherry and a dusty old bottle of Scotch whiskey Mr. Oglethorpe was saving for a special occasion.

Still puzzled, Theodora went to the kitchen to throw the tissues away. Mikko was standing at the counter, pounding an eggbeater handle-first into a bowl of eggs, shells and all. On the counter waiting to be added were a bag of mini-marshmallows and a jar of anchovy paste. Mikko stopped pounding the eggs and poured in half a cup each of whole peppercorns and chocolate sprinkles.

"It'll be ready in just a wink," she said to Theodora, smiling widely. Theodora took a startled step backward. For a split second, as if in a double exposure, she had seen Mikko's mouth full of small, even, round teeth, just like a doll's.

Then Theodora spotted Frankie. The cat was perched on the top of the refrigerator, back arched and every strand of his spotless white fur on end. His eyes were practically the size of Ping-Pong balls.

Theodora looked back at Mikko, who was pouring the egg mixture into a hot frying pan. Smoke began to fill the kitchen, along with a nasty smell of chocolate and anchovies. As Mikko began to poke at the omelette with the eggbeater, Theodora tiptoed back to her own room.

She flopped onto her bed and stared at the ceiling, where the pieces of duct tape that had held up the papier-mâché wyvern had taken patches of the paint with them. Whoever or *whatever* that thing in the kitchen was, it wasn't Mikko. Not even polish fumes or a nervous breakdown could account for such weird behavior.

The bedroom door squeaked as it was pushed open a crack, and Theodora sat up. It was Frankie. His fur was lying a little flatter, and his eyes were almost back to their usual size. He walked over to the bed and looked up at her forlornly, as if to say, *Well, what are we going to do?*

Theodora bent down and picked him up.

"I don't know, Frankie," she murmured into his fur. "But I'll think of something."

Frankie alone had witnessed what had happened when the delivery truck drove off. Mikko had signed for the large cardboard box, showing the deliveryman where to set it down in the hallway. As soon as Mikko turned her back to close the front door, Febrys had emerged from the box in her true form. In an instant the demon had changed into a cloud of cool, black smoke, winding around Mikko like a boa constrictor until it found a way in through her ears and nose. The possession complete, Febrys had given her new form a stretch and a shrug, wiggling her new jaw and flexing her fingers as though working them into a pair of tight gloves.

Then Febrys had discovered her new feet. Mikko had shapely feet and she took good care of them, gently scrubbing off calluses with a pumice stone and massaging them with peppermint foot cream. These were not human feet cobbled together by a lazy sorcerer using a shortcut incantation. These were the real thing. No more aching, cloven, demon feet wedged into human woman shoes.

"Beautiful feet!" she crooned to them.

Kobold's orders had been very clear: enter the Oglethorpe household, possess the human woman Michelle Kolodney, and gain the confidence of the Oglethorpe child with the aim of obtaining the wyvern trump. But all these instructions were soon very far from Febrys's mind.

Febrys had two traits that were most unfortunate in a demon: a weakness for pretty things and a short attention span. She wandered from room to room, pausing to study the framed snapshots of Andy Oglethorpe and

Theodora on the mantelpiece: at the zoology department's softball game, at the cabin in Maine, dressed up for Halloween as Dorothy and the Tin Man. Febrys noticed that the man in the photographs was always smiling. Kobold never smiled, at least not in a *nice* way.

Febrys opened her mouth and tried to laugh. It came out a tinny, faint "ha, ha" that hung in the room like a sad, leaky balloon. A few days ago a burst of sudden human laughter would have driven the demon into the nearest corner to hide. She drew in another breath and tried again, a louder "hahahaHAhaha" that was better.

Febrys was beginning to see what laughter could be for. It wasn't like a spell, exactly, but it had a power of its own.

Slowly a plan began to form in Febrys's stunted, demon mind, an idea like a tiny, frozen toad slowly uncurling in a bank of thawing mud. Then she wandered into Mikko's room, and there on the dressing table, sparkling in the light from the window, she saw a dozen tiny bottles of nail polish in all the colors of the rainbow.

Baby wyverns are extraordinarily large when they emerge from the egg. At hatching, they are already almost a third of their mother's weight and put on additional bulk very quickly. Within a day, Wycca's hatchling had opened its eyes and its rubbery beak had begun to harden. It raised its wobbly head and beat its small wings to strengthen them.

Wycca gave her baby a thorough sponge bath and decided that it was ready for its first flight, even if it would be only as a passenger. She needed to go foraging, and no wyvern mother would leave a nestling behind unguarded. Leaving a well-camouflaged egg for a few hours was one thing, but a young wyvern's cries might attract unwanted attention—animal, magical, or demonical.

She took off from the tower, the hatchling clinging to the scales of her belly with its long, well-developed claws. At the sudden rush of wind the newborn wyvern gave a snort of surprise and tightened its grip, pressing its face against Wycca's underbelly. When it realized it wasn't about to plummet to the ground, it gathered the courage to look down at the sights unrolling rapidly beneath them: the whale-watching boats heading back to Long Wharf, the hustle and bustle of the fruit and vegetable stalls at Haymarket, the throngs of tourists crowding the shopping arcade at Faneuil Hall.

They quickly left the busy harborfront behind, heading across the river. Wycca made good use of rising currents of air to take them higher and higher, out of the range of curious human eyes. She was banking for a turn that would take her over the New England Confectionary Company when she felt a sharp tug on her tail.

Wycca was so startled that she went into a free fall. Her frightened hatchling gave a cry of alarm and dug its claws more tightly into its mother. Wycca quickly recovered, and when she had reassured her passenger she twisted her head around to see what was on her tail.

It was no spell Gideon had ever taught her to corner, no imp or gremlin, either, and not even a common crow up to its usual, tiresome mischief. And it felt nothing like a Fetching. But there it was again, an unmistakable tug.

You don't have to be an experienced hacker to create havoc in a computer; a can of cola spilled over the keyboard will work just as well. In the same way, a simple stick in the spokes will topple over even the most expensive mountain bike. So it was that Theodora's unsophisticated incantation, nonsense words combined with rosemary smoke and the very real power of the wyvern trump, was enough to summon up a real spell. It was weak and clumsily made, and in fact it would have flunked any test of the Guild of Adepts in the Wizardly Arts for even elementary spellcasting. But it was a spell, all the same.

What made this spell troublesome for Wycca was that it was not a spell she knew. She could have made short work of a stronger and more expertly crafted spell, as long as it was one she recognized. But this spell was different. It was as though she had been exposed to some new kind of cold germ that she couldn't fight.

Soon the tug on her tail became a terrible heaviness that spread to her wings, making them feel as though they were made of lead. She could barely lift them into an upstroke.

The wyvern was losing altitude rapidly and had to struggle to steer clear of power lines and satellite dishes and chimneys as the streets of Cambridge loomed dangerously close. She would have to ditch, but where?

Just below, she spotted a small body of water, a pond with water lilies, not unlike the lilies in the moat at home, in her own Where and When. Wycca decided to make a water landing. Braking as hard as she could, the wyvern made for the small target. As the ground loomed nearer, Wycca felt her frantic hatchling loosen its hold as it tried to get a better grip on her scaly belly. That was all it took; before Wycca could grasp it in her talons, the hatchling was gone. Then she hit the pond.

Wycca could not have known the pool was a man-made lily pond only four feet deep. She cannonballed into it at just over twenty-five miles per hour, and the resulting splash emptied the pool, sending the water lilies and expensive Japanese carp flying high into the air.

Wycca hit the concrete bottom hard and felt a sickening snap in her right front leg. But the pain was nothing compared to her fear for her hatchling. The wyvern struggled to the side of the pool and called out sharply. There was an answering cry from the Oglethorpes' yard next door, partly screened from view by a thick stand of decorative bamboo.

The terrific splash had brought the owners of the house running. A woman was the first on the scene, gaping at the sight of a dozen carp flopping on the redwood deck. A man soon joined her, wearing only his boxer shorts, his face covered in shaving cream. They both stood and stared at the wreck of their lily pond, then started grabbing the wriggling, gasping fish.

They had just put the last carp in a makeshift tank made out of a garbage can when the woman grabbed her husband's arm and pointed to the back of the gardening shed next door.

"Honey! Something just disappeared around the corner of the Oglethorpes' shed!"

"It's only a cat. Or those kids again—they must have thrown a cherry bomb into the pond. This time I'm calling the cops."

He went back into the house. The woman turned to follow him, casting a backward glance at the shed. What she had seen was not a cat. Cats did not have *slithery* tails. But then, she didn't want to think about what did.

Wycca had slipped around the corner of the small shed. She called out once more for her baby, but the shock of the landing had left her stunned and disoriented. She turned this way and that, unable to pinpoint her baby's cry. But she did hear another sound: the sudden snap and metallic rattle of a chain giving way, then a dog's frantic barking growing louder and closer. Wycca turned and burrowed far beneath the shed, curling up in a nest used the previous spring by a family of skunks. She turned to face the canine intruder. A fiery blast would show him a thing or two!

But when Wycca tried to send a warning plume of flame toward the snarling muzzle, all that came out were some pitiful sparks. The dive into the carp pond had put out her fire. The dog was only startled, and Wycca had to stretch her neck to its full length and deliver a sharp bite to the creature's ear to get her message across. The dog turned and ran.

Wycca sank wearily onto the floor of the old skunk burrow, calling weakly to her baby, telling it she would come for it soon, when her strength had returned and her fire had rekindled.

This time there was no answering cry.

Theodora sat at the kitchen table, cautiously poking the anchovy-marshmallow-eggshell omelette on her plate. Across from her, Mikko looked up from her own lunch and frowned. She swallowed and asked, in a tone that suggested her feelings might be hurt, "What's wrong? Don't you like it?"

The thing on Theodora's plate was soft and yellow-gray, pockmarked with peppercorns and oozing anchovy-marshmallow filling. It looked almost exactly like the fake vomit Val had once slipped onto Milo's lunch tray at school back in the fourth grade.

"Oh, no, it smells *great,*" Theodora said. "I'm just not really very hungry for some reason. I did have a pretty big breakfast."

Mikko seemed satisfied with this explanation and took another crunchy bite. In her previous sham form the demon had had no need of nourishment, but now, in a real human body, she could at last enjoy food and drink as she had seen humans do. She swallowed with gusto and washed the hideous mouthful down with a large gulp of apple juice.

Demons have a real sweet tooth, and Theodora had taken one sip from her own glass only to discover that the juice had been sweetened with about half a plastic bear of honey and a generous squirt of lemon dish-washing liquid. Mikko/Febrys had discovered she could take a sip and then blow out a stream of iridescent bubbles. This delighted and distracted her so much that Theodora was able to slip from her chair unnoticed and make her way out into the backyard.

Ever since she was old enough to climb it, the big copper beech in the backyard had been Theodora's thinking tree, the place she went when she needed to be alone. She hadn't climbed it so much lately, but her feet remembered where all the good toeholds were. In the secret mossy hollow where the trunk diverged, she felt around for the smooth, heart-shaped stone she had placed there three summers before. Turning it over in her hands, Theodora wondered what to do.

She wished her father wasn't off in the jungles of Laos. She could send him a fax or a telegram, but what could she say? That Mikko had been kidnapped and some creepy alien thing was pretending to be her? Oh, *that* would bring him home in a hurry.

Two fat tears rolled down Theodora's cheeks and splashed onto the stone. She wiped them away.

Thinking thoughts like these, it wasn't surprising that Theodora did not notice the men who approached the Oglethorpe house and walked up the front path.

There were two of them. The first was older, shorter, and grayer, dressed too warmly for a summer's day. His sleeves were rolled up, and he had a tweed jacket with leather elbow patches draped over one arm. The second man was younger and taller, and carried himself in a way that suggested he was a stranger a long way from home.

The little roly-poly man raised a furled umbrella and used its tip to ring the doorbell. After a minute he rang the bell again, then crouched down on the front step to peer through the mail slot. He and his companion exchanged a few words, and then the taller and younger of the pair took a few steps toward the side of the house, shaking his head, before allowing his friend to take his arm and lead him back toward the street.

15

The Rescue

"I TELL YOU, MERLIN, I felt it, right *here*." Gideon thumped his chest with his fist. "Wycca was very near—I know it."

"That may well be, but I tell you, my friend, I *smelled* it, right here," replied Merlin, tapping his nose. "The unmistakable whiff of Demon First Class. Besides, you can't stroll into someone's backyard uninvited. It just isn't done."

The walk back into Harvard Square had been warm, and the two wizards had paused at a corner store, where Merlin purchased bottles of lemonade. They drank them sitting on a bench on the lawn of the public library, watching a man tossing a Frisbee to his dog. Now a silence fell over the pair as they both thought dark thoughts about demons, the missing wyvern trump card, and the fate of Gideon's wyvern.

Gideon finished his own lemonade and looked up. "But what has befallen Theodora Oglethorpe?"

"I have been thinking about that. There are, as I see it, four likely scenarios. One, she may be in the house with the demon, unaware of the danger. Two, she may be imprisoned in the house. Three, she may have discovered the danger and made her escape. Four—"

"She may herself be possessed by the demon," said Gideon.

"Yes," said Merlin. "That was number four."

Another silence fell over them, even gloomier than the one before. At last Merlin spoke.

"Meter readers."

Gideon dragged his attention from the Frisbee game. He had been thinking that it would make a useful device for training wyverns.

"Meter readers," Merlin repeated. "Natural gas company inspectors. Animal control officers—what they used to call, in my long-ago boyhood, dogcatchers."

Gideon waited patiently. He had learned that Merlin's cryptic utterances were usually followed by explanations.

Merlin slapped his knee, tipping over the rest of his lemonade.

"That's it! My good Gideon, they are all officials whose occupations allow them access to private property. Such as Theodora Oglethorpe's backyard. Now, let's make our way back to the apartment, and I'll do a little reading up in *F.S.S.S.B. IV* about driving out demons—First, Second, or Third Class."

Theodora stayed up in the thinking tree for a long time, long enough to cry out all the scared weepiness and the awful, achy missing of her dad so she could go back into the house and face the Mikko-that-wasn't. She had decided she couldn't put it off any longer and had started to swing one foot down to the next branch when she realized she was still clutching the smooth, heart-shaped stone.

She held it in her open palm for a minute, about to just toss it away, but changed her mind. After all, she had thrown a lot of things away already today; it wouldn't hurt to hold on to one small stone. Besides, the way her luck had been going, her dad wouldn't get a permanent job and they'd be leaving this house and this yard and this tree. Theodora reached back into the secret hollow to return it to its hiding place.

This time, as she reached into the mossy crevice, something curled up among the dried leaves and half-gnawed acorns bit her.

Theodora snatched back her hand, too startled to make a sound. She wiggled her fingers cautiously but could see no punctures, just an angry red mark where her hand had received a sharp pinch.

She leaned back against the wide branch and blinked. Maybe it was a baby squirrel, left behind when the others departed the nest. Or a baby robin that hadn't learned to fly. But it didn't *smell* like a nest—it didn't have that funky hamster-cage-overdue-for-cleaning smell—and there weren't tufts of down or fur caught in the bark around the opening.

Dad would just kill me if he knew what I'm going to do, she thought, slipping off one sneaker and using the sock from that foot to protect her hand. Trying not to think of rabies, she used the sneaker as bait, lowering it toe-first into the hole and wiggling it provocatively to get the occupant's attention. When she felt something bite and hold on, she reached in with her sock-covered hand and grabbed the creature squirming at the very bottom of the nest cavity.

It was much too large to be a baby squirrel and there were more than two legs kicking against her grasping hand, and they didn't feel spindly and birdlike. But it wasn't until she had a good grip on the struggling animal and had hauled it out into the light that Theodora realized what it was.

Imagine a creature as sleek and muscular as a young

otter but covered all over in dark, almost metallic scales, with a beak where its whiskered muzzle ought to be and stubby, baby-bat wings, and you have some idea of the animal Theodora held—or did her best to hold—in her arms. The hatchling looked up at her with wide, yellow eyes and croaked.

Theodora was so shocked to find herself holding a real, live baby wyvern that she almost dropped it. She started to say "Omigod" but all that came out was "Oh!"

"Wroa," said the wyvern.

Theodora put out a hand and cautiously scratched it on its head and on the underside of its beak (which was the closest thing it had to a chin).

"It's all right," she told it. "It's okay. You're safe now."

The wyvernling stopped struggling and settled into the position instinct told it was the most secure: spread-eagle on Theodora's chest like a mountain climber on a cliff face, clinging to her T-shirt with its sharp claws.

Theodora's mind was racing. She could not keep the wyvern in the house, not as long as the Mikko-that-wasn't was there. But where could she keep it, hidden from neighbors, stray dogs, and suburban raccoons? She would have to think of something before it got dark.

And she would have to figure out what to feed it. It was obviously not ready to be taken from its mother, and something told her that even the enormous Pet-O-Rama out at the Galleria didn't carry cans of wyvern milk in the pet food aisle. In the movie *Wizards & Wyverns,* the apprentice wyvernkeeper fed the baby wyvern a mixture of cat's milk and honey, but Theodora looked at the baby wyvern and thought the scriptwriter had probably made that up. She just couldn't imagine Frankie putting up with a milking, even if he'd been a Francine.

But the thought of Mikko's cat put a plan into her head. Theodora pried the wyvern's claws loose from her T-shirt and gently returned the baby to its hiding place.

"Stay here," she told it. "Don't worry, I'll be right back."

She was able to creep back into the house undetected and quietly gather everything she needed from the basement and kitchen. When she had finished these preparations Theodora went to find the Mikko-that-wasn't. She found the imposter trying on Mikko's red silk Chinese slippers. Shoes—from clogs to black-satin tango shoes and everything in between—were strewn all over the floor of Mikko's room.

Theodora stood in the doorway, her school backpack slung over one shoulder and Frankie's cat carrier clutched in one hand.

"Bye. I'm going now."

The Mikko-that-wasn't swiveled her head around, looking at once suspicious and dismayed.

"Going? Where? Why?"

Theodora wrinkled her brow. "Don't you remember? We talked about it this morning." She hefted the cat carrier. "I'm taking Frankie to the vet and then I'm spending the night at Val's house." When this failed to get a reaction, Theodora rolled her eyes. "Val? Valerie van der Zeek? My best friend who was over here, like, *yesterday?*"

Mikko/Febrys's small demon brain struggled to take in the foreign concepts of *vet, spend the night,* and *best friend.* She would have to ask Kobold what they meant. But she recalled her master's advice: *When in doubt, nod and smile.* Fixing her teeth in the position she had practiced so faithfully in front of the mirror, the demon nodded and bared her teeth.

"Fine!" she said brightly. "Fine!"

She was still saying "Fine!" as Theodora let herself out the back door.

As soon as she was outside, Theodora let Frankie out of the cat carrier and into the Oglethorpes' basement through the window she'd opened earlier. She'd left bowls of cat food and water for him.

"Please don't howl," she pleaded, "or else she'll know you're here. I'll come back for you." Then she removed the stick propping open the window and let it drop shut and latch.

This time when she reached for it, the wyvern trembled but did not bite. Theodora let the hatchling get a good grip on her chest and then started down the beech tree. Once they were safely on the ground, she carefully unhooked the clawed feet from her T-shirt and gently transferred the wyvern to the cat carrier, which she had lined with an old towel.

"It'll be okay," she said to it through the wire mesh door. "I'm taking you someplace where you'll be safe."

She strapped the cat carrier onto the back of her mountain bike. Theodora hadn't realized how much she'd grown since the spring—the bike seemed too small for her, and her longer legs made it awkward to pedal.

As she rode Theodora wished with all her might that the hideout would still be there.

Febrys sat on the floor of Mikko's room, surrounded by shoes. She was suddenly tired of trying them on, and there was a strange pain in her stomach, which she thought must be a punishment sent by Kobold. The demon had no way of knowing that if you ate something peculiar, it was likely to disagree with you. Marshmallow-anchovy omelettes and detergent apple juice are certainly peculiar, and they were definitely disagreeing with the demon's new human digestion. Febrys gathered up all the shoes and shoved them in a jumbled pile back into the closet.

She wandered through the house, rubbing her stomach and wondering what she would tell Kobold if he appeared and asked where the child was. Her master had sent her to look for the wyvern trump. Perhaps if she found it, he would not be angry that she had let the Oglethorpe girl leave the house. If he was angry, he might make her change her shape back to the ill-fitting human woman form.

Febrys began to search the house, looking for the purse that the human woman Michelle Kolodney had carried at the bookstore of Giles and Moira Hatch. She remembered that it was made from a piece of tapestry and had a length of fine brass chain for a handle. At last Febrys spotted it, tucked high on the top shelf of the linen closet. She reached up and hooked her fingers through the chain and pulled the purse down.

But she had no sooner caught the purse in her hands then the demon dropped it with a howl and stuck her fingers in her mouth, whimpering with pain. When she took her fingers out again, they were beginning to blister. The purse had burned her, though it had not felt hot. Something about it had given her a magical scalding.

The purse lay on the floor. There was nothing remarkable about the pattern, at least not the part of it that was lying faceup: a background of leaves and flowers into which were woven hunting dogs in endless pursuit of a rabbit. Mikko/Febrys reached out cautiously with her foot and flipped the bag over. When she saw the design that was woven into the tapestry on the other side, she let loose a shriek of fright and ran away down the hall.

Mikko had purchased the handbag five summers earlier, on an art tour through medieval towns in France. The fabric was a cheap reproduction of the famous tapestry of the lady and the unicorn, with the captured unicorn resting its head in the lap of a beautiful maiden. Virtuous young women and unicorns are both powerful charms against the darker varieties of magic. If it had borne the words SORCERERS AND DEMONS KEEP OUT, in large red letters, Mikko's bag couldn't have been any more secure against thievery—at least by demon hands.

Febrys was still cowering in the kneehole under Mr. Oglethorpe's desk when two men in tan jumpsuits boldly made their way up the Oglethorpes' driveway and into the backyard. Embroidered on the backs of their jumpsuits were the words ANIMAL CONTROL. One man (whose jumpsuit was a little too small for him) was carrying a large net, while his companion was lugging a black plastic case that resembled an oversized fishing tackle box.

Gideon set down the tackle box at the foot of the copper beech tree and stood shading his eyes, gazing up into the spreading branches. Merlin stood respectfully to one side. Like most modern wizards, he had no practical experience of wyverns and other dragons, so it was a rare opportunity to watch a wyvernmaster at work.

Gideon soon spotted Theodora's worn footholds in the bark, and it didn't take him long to climb to the spot where the massive trunk split into two branches. This was not a place a wyvern would choose to hatch an egg—only the most dire peril could have compelled Wycca to leave her nestling here. That is, if she had. Separated from its mother, a wyvernling will seek out the nearest dark, secret place; the nestling might well have crawled here on its own.

Gideon reached into the mossy crevice and lifted out a large handful of matted moss and twigs, which he stowed in a bag at his waist. He then slid back down the trunk and swung from the last branch onto the ground, without loosening a single leaf on the tree.

He spread out the contents of the pouch for Merlin to see. Aside from the moss, there was a handful of acorn shells, a heart-shaped stone, and something else that would have escaped Merlin's attention entirely. It was about the size of the nail on your little finger but wider at one end than the other and far stronger. It seemed glossy black at first, but as Gideon turned it in the palm of his hand the sunlight hit it, and it suddenly winked like a prism, flashing streaks of purple and silver and green.

"A wyvern scale!" cried Merlin. "I never thought to see one. Virtually indestructible, aren't they? Impervious to fire, acid, arrows, et cetera? Wouldn't the brass at the

Pentagon like to spend a few days with *this* in the lab."

Gideon did not ask what the Pentagon was. He was examining the scale. "It is not Wycca's," he said. "It is not worn enough along the edge. It is the scale from a hatchling—her hatchling. But it could not have made its way far from the tree without help."

He kneeled on the grass beside the tackle box and unfastened the latches that held it shut. Inside, neatly arranged in the compartments, were the coil of mermaid's hair, the golden bridle, and the dragon mint wyvern treats, as well as some props Merlin had felt essential to their successful masquerade as animal control officers: a flashlight, a small field guide to animal tracks, and a large tin box of Skunk-B-Gone that looked suspiciously like paprika. Ignus was confined inside an empty aftershave bottle that had been relabeled BAT REPELLANT, EXTRA STRENGTH, and Ouroboros was neatly coiled up alongside the mermaid's-hair rope.

Gideon removed a small piece of leather—all that was left of the shoe that had been Wycca's security blanket when she was a yearling just beginning her training. She had reduced the shoe to a mere scrap of hide, pierced by her sharp beak so it almost had the appearance of lace. The wizard took a dragon treat and folded the scrap of leather around it. Like a message in a bottle, it would tell Wycca that he had been here and would return. He left the small bundle under some leaves at the foot of the copper beech. As he straightened up Gideon put his hand to his heart and winced, leaning against the tree for support. Merlin stepped forward to take his arm.

"Gideon! What is it?"

"Again—I feel it—she is near. But it is much fainter." Gideon looked around the yard, spied the tool-shed, and thought of Wycca's old hiding place under the castle dovecote. He slowly circled the shed and stopped by the corner where the earth had been clawed away to widen the entrance to an animal's burrow.

Gideon lay flat on the grass and used the flashlight to peer into the tunnel. It dropped away steeply, then hooked sharply to the left. The tunnel bore no clues: no wyvern tracks, no shimmering black scales. It smelled strongly of skunk.

Gideon sat up, handing the flashlight to Merlin.

"I cannot tell. I believe she *must* be there, but perhaps it is only that I wish it so. I fear she is in danger, gravely wounded or beset by spells as perilous."

Merlin snapped his fingers. "I may have thought of something. Couldn't we send our good friend Ouroboros down the tunnel? If Wycca is holed up in there, he could report her condition and even take her medicine in the form of a doctored dragon treat."

At first this did seem to be the answer to their problem, and Ouroboros gamely ventured down the burrow.

But he quickly slithered back out, nearly losing an inch of his tail as he beat a retreat. He emerged from the burrow a little singed, but not too worse for wear.

As Merlin tried to remove some of the soot, Ouroboros observed a little wryly that at least they knew it was a dragon in the burrow and not a skunk.

Ouroboros was willing to try again, but Gideon feared that the next time Wycca struck out blindly, she might injure or even kill the snake. There was a limit to what a spell could do to protect Ouroboros from a desperate dragon. In the end, they agreed it would be safe to leave the snake at the entrance to the burrow as a sentry. Gideon left Ouroboros under an overturned flowerpot just outside the opening to the skunk burrow.

During all this Wycca lay out of sight at the far end of the skunk burrow under the toolshed, only a few yards away. Pain had forced the injured wyvern to withdraw deep into herself, and the powerful stink of skunk kept her from detecting her master's familiar scent or recognizing Ouroboros. She lay in a heap, hungry and thirsty and crazed with pain, rousing herself only to cry feebly to her hatchling.

16

Sanctuary

ALL THE WAY from Oxford Street to Sacramento, the creature in the cat carrier kept up a pitiful moaning. Theodora tried to pedal without too many jolts over curbs, but she could hear the baby wyvern clawing and tugging at the small wire grate in the carrier door. The *wroas* were getting more desperate, but with the carrier strapped behind her, there wasn't much she could do to comfort it.

The red light at the corner of Massachusetts Avenue took forever, and while she was waiting for it to change, she had to warn away a father and his little girl who wanted to take a peek at the "kitty in the box."

"I wouldn't get too close," she said, twisting around on the seat to cover the grate with her hand before they could get a good look. "She's got striped swamp tick fever, and it's *highly* contagious."

As the man scooped up his daughter and hurried away with her down the sidewalk, the light finally turned green and Theodora sped across the street. Here the houses were a whole lot fancier than in her own neighborhood—some had turrets and stained-glass windows, and the lawns and the gardens were the kind you usually see only in magazines.

This was the part of Cambridge where Milo had lived with his mother and Milo's first stepfather, who was supposed to do something with other people's money but hadn't done it very well. They hadn't lived in one of the fancy houses but in the Agassiz Arms, a sprawling brick apartment building that had been built to resemble a medieval castle. Milo called it the Saggy Arms. He used to joke that the roof had crenellations—those square teeth around the roofline of a castle—so the apartment dwellers could pour boiling oil down onto door-to-door salespeople. Milo knew a lot of words like *crenellations* (not to mention *quagga* and *zax*), so that few people were willing to play Scrabble with him more than once.

For a while this last winter, perhaps because they all

knew they would soon be too old for it, Theodora, Val, and Milo had met in a secret clubhouse high up under the roof of the apartment building. Milo had discovered a narrow stairway that led from the old coal cellar in the basement up to an abandoned storage room under the eaves.

It was a clubhouse without a club—at least, their club didn't have a name or password. They were the only members, and their meetings consisted of aimless conversations about nothing in particular and the consumption of their official club snack, gummi bears.

Theodora hid her bike behind a hedge and found the hinged door that covered the coal chute. She always felt a little shiver before she closed her eyes and slid down into the cool, dark cellar, visions of black widow spiders dancing in her head. Now she clucked some encouragement to the baby wyvern and gently sent the cat carrier down the chute into the darkness. She heard the carrier hit the bottom and slid down after it, clutching her backpack.

The carrier had landed upside down at the bottom of the coal chute, and with her heart beating wildly, she turned it right side up and peered in through the metal grate. Two large, yellow eyes blinked back at her, and instead of a *wroa,* it gave a hiss—not unlike the one Frankie made when Mikko and Theodora took him to the vet to get his teeth cleaned. She let out a big sigh. If it was mad enough to hiss, it couldn't have been hurt that badly.

It took all of her strength to move the heavy crate blocking the door that led up to the box room, but at last she managed to shove it to one side. At the top of the narrow staircase, Theodora set the carrier down on the landing and felt along the dusty ledge over the door. The key was still there, and it still opened the door. It had occurred to her on the ride over that the janitor might have found what was left of their clubhouse and changed the lock.

It was all just as they had left it, from the dead wasps on the windowsill of the small, octagonal window to the broken stone gargoyle peeking out from under the hood of the old wicker baby buggy. Their milk-crate stools were still pulled up around the old steamer trunk they had used as a table. Stuck to the lid of the trunk was a small green puddle Theodora finally recognized as a pile of rejected green gummi bears, which had melted like the Wicked Witch in the summer heat.

Theodora set the carrier down on the floor and opened it. The baby wyvern poked the tip of its beak into the strange room, then stuck its whole head out. Theodora talked to it softly as she lit a candle and began to unload her backpack, setting out a thermos, a funnel, an empty plastic soda bottle, a rubber glove, and several bottles taken from the Oglethorpe pantry.

"Hang on," she told it, "I'm going to fix you something to eat. Everything'll be okay." Although she thought, as she began to pour milk from the thermos through the funnel into the soda bottle, that it couldn't possibly understand her, and even if it did, it probably didn't believe her. Because Theodora wasn't at all sure that everything *was* going to be okay, and her hand shook just a little as she started to pour corn syrup down the funnel.

The wyvern made its way on wobbly legs over to where Theodora sat cross-legged on the floor, concocting a batch of what she hoped would pass for wyvern milk. The hatchling sat down on its haunches and watched the proceedings with great seriousness, then suddenly set about giving its scales a vigorous preening.

Back in the penthouse overlooking the Public Garden, Kobold had just finished a late lunch—lobster bisque, filet mignon, and a passion-fruit soufflé, all summoned by spellcraft out from under the nose of the astonished chef at the Four Seasons Hotel next door. It was a far cry from the fare he'd eaten at the tables of the various lesser nobles and warlords who had employed him—half-spoiled boar meat that no amount of spices or sorcery could really improve, and watered-down wine.

Once he had delivered to his master either Gideon or proof of his destruction, Kobold would be able to claim his reward. He dwelled with pleasure on the many things, beginning with spoiled boar's meat, that he would put far behind him, when he was no longer a mere wizard-for-hire.

A sudden unbidden thought intruded on his reverie: he imagined his master's voice saying coolly in quicksilver tones, "So he has neither been delivered nor destroyed? Can you explain this?"

Kobold hastily thrust the unwelcome thought away and drained the rest of his wine, blotted his lips with a fine linen napkin, and reached for the remote control.

In general he found the flat-screen television a great improvement over a crystal ball. It had taken him only a few attempts, and some minor adjustments to the usual spell, to get the screen to function in the same manner. But now, as he tuned in to see what progress his demon was making in her quest for the wyvern trump, he did not like the image he saw splashed in vivid color on the wall of the living room. Pressing the buttons of the remote, he clicked from room to room of the Oglethorpe house as though he were changing channels. The child was nowhere to be seen, and it was only after several passes that he spied Febrys's feet sticking out from under a desk.

For a moment the computer monitor on Andy Oglethorpe's desk buzzed as Kobold attempted to bring it to life. The spell he used was one of the group of fly-on-the-wall incantations, something every wizard had to master. Properly performed, it allowed one to project one's likeness on a surface, usually still water or a mirror. But no matter how much Kobold buzzed, the screen remained dark. At last he cursed and used a different spell to turn the computer mouse into a real mouse, tethered to the computer by its long tail. His nose twitched with annoyance and when he spoke, Kobold's voice came out in an undignified squeak.

"Febrys!"

The demon crept out from under the desk and scrambled to her feet, expecting to find her master in the room, only to discover his eyes scowling at her from the mouse.

"I found the wyvern trump, master," she said, wringing her hands. "But it stung my fingers when I tried to take it."

"That is because the girl must give it to you of her own will—as I explained to you. Where is the child?"

"She has gone to the best vet's night to spend the house," stammered the demon. "I mean, the best night's spend to house the friend—"

"Enough," snapped Kobold. "Remain there in case the child returns. I will deal with you later, once I have had a chance to consider what *form* your punishment should take." With that the eyes on the mouse squeezed themselves shut tight and vanished, though it took another minute for the whiskers to completely disappear.

Febrys did not like the way he had said the word *form.* Once before when she had earned his displeasure, Kobold had turned her into the sooty cauldron in which the apothecary brewed batches of eye ointment. Even when she had been allowed to resume her sham human form, it had been weeks before she could scrub the soot off the back of her neck and get the nasty taste of ointment out of her mouth.

Ouroboros waited all afternoon under the flowerpot. He slept a little, and to pass the time between naps, he ran through the family tree of the kings and queens of England in one head while he did quadratic equations in the other. Such mental calisthenics kept his memory nimble.

As the shadows grew longer, the snake yawned and poked his heads out from under the flowerpot, tasting the air with his two forked tongues. The smells were complex—skunk, of course, and underneath that, like the layers of an onion, other, fainter scents: charcoal briquettes and lighter fluid, fabric softener from the clothes dryer running in the basement of the house next door, tanning lotion from the teenage boy sunbathing four houses down. And underneath all of those was another smell, one that didn't immediately register in the snake's memory. He flicked his tongues once more, gathering up atoms of scent, and tried again.

Now there flashed into his heads a rapid succession of images: Maya warriors in brilliantly feathered headdresses, drinking from golden cups before a battle; a French countess in a towering white wig and enormous skirts being brought a silver pot on a tray by an African slave; the dedication of a large factory in Hershey, Pennsylvania.

"Chocolate. Of course," said Ouroboros. "And it's coming from that burrow. Well, if Wycca has developed a taste for the food of the gods, no dried-up piece of rabbit jerky will coax her out of there." He shook his heads.

It was the vibrations felt through his coils that alerted Ouroboros to movement in the skunk burrow. He slipped out from under the safety of the flowerpot and slithered down the entrance until he could just peer around the bend to the main chamber.

Wycca lay on a pile of leaves in obvious distress, her eyes half shut and her beak agape. There were flecks of sickly foam at the corners of her mouth. She looked at the snake without a flicker of either recognition or alarm in her glazed eyes. One of her legs lay useless, bent at an unnatural angle.

Ouroboros quietly backed out of the chamber. At the burrow's entrance he met the real owner. She had been peacefully asleep in the burrow when Wycca had crawled into it, and the skunk hadn't taken kindly to being awakened in the middle of her "night" and forced to move into the spare bedroom until the sun went down and her nocturnal "day" began. But now she positively drew the line at a two-headed snake.

"No, no, no!" said the snake, as the female skunk swung around and prepared to spray. "That won't help matters. If you want this dragon out of your den, listen to me. You of all creatures must know where I can get some chocolate."

The skunk stifled a yawn. She had no use for chocolate, not when there were chicken bones and melon rinds to be had. But the skunk really did want her den back, and if she had to help out a two-headed snake in order to evict the sharp-beaked squatter, well, so be it.

Theodora had based her recipe for wyvern formula on a story she has seen on TV about a woman who helped to raise orphaned zoo animals. She couldn't remember the actual recipe, but she knew it contained a lot of fat and sugar in addition to milk, so she'd mixed together equal parts of milk, corn syrup, and Mikko's best olive oil (which she really didn't think the Mikko-that-wasn't would miss). She'd fastened a finger from the rubber glove on the end of the plastic bottle to serve as a nipple and had been thrilled when the baby wyvern eagerly fastened on to it, sucking vigorously.

Then it gagged and spit it out, all over Theodora.

She tried again, first with less oil and more syrup, and then more oil and less syrup, but each time the baby wyvern gagged and spit. In the end, it turned its head and wouldn't even take the nipple in its beak.

By now Theodora was hot and exhausted and covered in wyvern spit-up, which smelled a lot worse than the wyvern formula that had gone into the hatchling. Tears of frustration stung her eyes, and she tried to keep from giving in to a rising sense of panic. What if she should have left the wyvern where it was? Maybe its mother would have come back for it after all. What if she couldn't get it to eat anything? How long would it take it to starve?

For about the ninety-ninth time that day, she wished that her father wasn't thousands of miles away in the jungles of Laos. He would have known what to do. Theodora racked her brains. Whom could she trust? Not Gina at Traveler's Tales, not Giles and Moira, not even her fifth-grade science teacher, Mrs. Lohavani (who was pretty cool, considering). Everyone would tell her to turn the wyvern over to a zoo, and something told Theodora that would be the end of the wyvern.

Then she thought of the perfect person. She put the hatchling back in the carrier and locked the box room door behind her. In her spit-up-covered T-shirt and jeans, she rode to the nearest Laundromat with a pay phone (Andy Oglethorpe stubbornly insisted that no eleven-year-old needed a cell phone). She got the number from information, and then the pay phone swallowed her money. Frantically, Theodora fished in the lint deep in her jeans pocket, and found enough change for another call.

One ring. Two rings. Oh, pleasepleaseplease be home . . . Oh please, she silently pleaded.

"Hello?"

Theodora was so relieved, she almost dropped the receiver.

"Dr. Naga?" Suddenly, she could barely talk around the lump in her throat, and the words came out in shaky gasps. "It's me, Theodora. Theodora Oglethorpe."

"My dear! Whatever is the matter?"

"Oh, Dr. Naga! Can you come right away?"

Febrys sat in the kneehole under Andy Oglethorpe's desk, deep in thought—or as deep in thought as a demon with a very shallow brain can be.

Kobold was certain to arrive any minute, and an unpleasant punishment would not be far behind. The demon liked this new form, especially the shapely feet with a slender heel and toes she could actually wiggle. She did not intend to give it up without a fight. But how could she hope to outwit her master, who was as strong and cruel as he was clever?

On the corner of the desk there was a sleek black

gadget that came to life from time to time, speaking in different voices and winking with its green eye. Now it chirruped loudly, and on the third chirrup the girl's voice came out through dozens of tiny holes in the top of the instrument.

"Hi! You've reached the Oglethorpe household. If you want to leave a message for Andy, press one. If you want to leave a message for *me,* Theodora, press two. And if you want to leave a message for Mikko or Frankie, press three. Here comes the beep!"

Now a disembodied male voice came through the little holes.

"Theodora, are you there? It's me, Daddy. Listen, I've tried to get through a couple of times. I hope you're not on-line all the time in one of your dragon chat rooms. Anyway, tell Mikko I'm calling from—"

A violent crackle of static wiped out the rest of the sentence, and when it subsided the voice was faint and distorted.

"—on my way," it said.

The voice fell silent and the green eye began to wink steadily. Febrys did not like the winking eye, and she had learned that, by pressing some of the buttons on the top of the device, she could make it stop winking.

She had just stretched out a finger to do this when a hand reached out and grabbed her wrist.

The demon jumped back and gave a little shriek. It

was Kobold. She cowered, holding her free hand in front of her face, but no stinging spell was hurled her way. The wizard was too busy examining the answering machine.

He had brought along the white remote from the penthouse, but when he pointed it at the apparatus and pressed the large green button, nothing happened. It apparently had no power over this contrivance. The wizard scrutinized the words printed on the answering-machine buttons, murmuring to himself.

"Delete . . . repeat . . . stop . . . skip . . . play," he said slowly. He pressed PLAY and listened to Andy Oglethorpe's message. It took only a simple spell—one usually used to eavesdrop through thick castle walls—to clear up the static crackle.

"Anyway, tell Mikko I'm calling from the airport," the voice said clearly. "As soon as I can catch a cab, I'm on my way."

Kobold bit the knuckles of his left hand nervously. An airport was perhaps to ships of the air what a seaport was to ships of the sea. He had seen such craft overhead. But what a cab might be and how one caught one were a mystery (he had made his way across the river to Cambridge in a limousine spirited, with its driver, from the garage of the Four Seasons Hotel). But the last words, "I'm on my way," could only mean one thing.

Kobold pressed more buttons, replaying the old

messages Febrys hadn't erased. Voices, young and old, male and female, came through the speaker holes in jumbled phrases: "I ran to the store and got stuck in traffic. . . . I'll be right back in a few minutes. . . . seemed pretty worked up about it . . . deadline for the mid-term . . . Yes? Who is this? . . . Would you like to hold?"

The wizard began to see how it could be done. He glanced at Febrys, who was still cringing.

"Stop cowering and listen."

17

The Care and Feeding of Young Wyverns

A LOUD GURGLE AND sigh signaled the end of the brew cycle for a third pot of coffee. Merlin rose stretching from his chair, picked up the two empty mugs, and carried them out into the kitchen.

They had drawn two armchairs up to Merlin's desk, its heavy oak surface covered with books—not only *F.S.S.S.B. IV* but *F.S.S.S.B. II* and *III*, as well as a stack of books with such titles as *A Field Guide to Demons of the New World* and *Driving Away Demons in Thirteen Easy Steps.* There was even an old hardcover book, stamped DISCARD by the Salem Public Library and purchased by Merlin for fifteen cents back in 1972, titled *Demons Dispelled: The Modern Approach.* To judge from the illustrations, the "modern approach" involved a costume that was a cross between a beekeeper's outfit and an early space suit, and a metal detector retrofitted to pick up traces of demon saliva. (Demons in their true form tend to drool uncontrollably.)

Merlin set the mugs down and went back to his perusal of *Demons for Dummies.* At the other end of the table, Gideon had let his own book fall shut and was staring into space.

"Merlin."

"Hmm?"

"The oracle of the Ouija. You said it could not be used to track a wyvern, especially one that did not want to be found."

"Mmm-hmm."

"But is it always so? Could it not tell us where to find a wyvern too young to know such wiles? If it cannot lead us to Wycca, perhaps it could tell us where to find her hatchling."

Merlin looked up from his book. The younger wizard's eyes had a bright gleam to them.

"Perhaps," he said thoughtfully. "Perhaps. We've been at this for hours. I suppose it won't hurt to take a break."

They set up the board on the coffee table, and this time Gideon himself addressed the oracle.

"Oh, Great Oracle, tell us where to find the hatchling of the wyvern named Wycca, familiar to your faithful servant Gideon."

The planchette began to move beneath their fingers. It rolled smoothly over to the number 8 and rolled no farther.

The two wizards waited for a few minutes, but the planchette stubbornly stayed right where it was.

"Ask it again," said Merlin. "In a slightly different way and with a pinch of flattery this time."

"No, you," said Gideon. "It answered you before."

They set the planchette in the middle of the board, and Merlin cleared his throat and said, "Oh, Mighty Ouija, Greatest of All Oracles, we beseech you to tell us the precise location of the hatchling of the wyvern named Wycca, the familiar of your most faithful and abject servant Gideon."

This time the planchette lingered at number 8, then went on to a series of letters.

"T-H-F-L-O-O," said Merlin. "What in creation is a *thfloo?*"

"Wait," said Gideon. "It yet moves."

At last the planchette came to a stop.

"R," said Merlin. "That makes *floor* so 8-T-H must be *eighth.* But eighth-floor *where* is the question. It can't mean this building. It doesn't go any higher than seven."

"Perhaps there is a hidden room," said Gideon. His own king's castle was honeycombed with secret chambers and false walls.

Merlin sat bolt upright and snapped his fingers. "Not hidden, my friend. But almost certainly forgotten. Two years ago all the residents of the Agassiz Arms were assessed a fee for the removal of a family of little brown bats from an old box room under the eaves. If bats could get in, a wyvern certainly could."

Dr. Naga picked Theodora up outside the Laundromat in a tiny, ancient green car. From a large tote bag on the backseat, she took a clean T-shirt and a wet washcloth in a plastic bag and gave them to Theodora, who was able to get off the worst of the wyvern spit-up. There was also a thermos of tea, milky and sweet with Indian spices. After a few sips Theodora was feeling much better, and the whole story poured out of her in one long, breathless burst.

Dr. Naga listened without comment to Theodora's description of finding the wyvern card stuck to her shoe, the visit to Giles and Moira's bookstore, meeting Mr. Lambton and Ms. Worm, her fight with Mikko and Mikko's transformation into the Mikko-that-wasn't, finding the baby wyvern, and all the rest. When Theodora was finished Dr. Naga only said,

"And you have left this creature in the box room?"

"Yes."

"Take me to it."

When they got to the apartment building, there was nowhere to park, and they ended up circling the block for fifteen minutes, while Dr. Naga shook her head.

"My parking karma must be on the blink. How very tiresome," she said. "Ah! Here is one, at last."

A blue Volvo was just pulling out of a spot, and Dr. Naga slipped the little green car into the space.

As they got out, Theodora noticed for the first time that Dr. Naga wasn't wearing a sari but a more practical outfit of a dark T-shirt and carpenter's jeans. When they got to the coal chute she produced from one of her many pockets a small, powerful flashlight. Theodora's surprise must have shown on her face, because Dr. Naga looked at her and laughed.

"I thought it best to come prepared. When I was in college in Kentucky many years ago, we used to go spelunking."

"What's spelunking?"

"Messing about in caves. My boyfriend at the time was a very avid caver, and because I was small, I managed to slip through passages the others couldn't. I learned to dress for tight squeezes through small, dark spaces and always to carry a good flashlight. It has come in handy many times since."

Luckily no one had moved the packing crate back in front of the staircase. They made it up to the box room without any trouble, but when Theodora felt along the sill over the door for the key, she was almost certain it wasn't in the same spot on the narrow ledge. A sudden feeling of dread made her stomach do a flip-flop, and she fumbled to get the key into the old lock. At last she got the door open, only to let out a wail of dismay at the sight before her.

In the time it had taken Dr. Naga to drive all the way from Salem, fetch Theodora at the Laundromat, listen to her story, and then find a place to park, someone had beaten them to the box room. An empty cat carrier, its door wide open, sat in the middle of the floor. There was no sign of the wyvern.

They searched the box room just to be sure. Dr. Naga found the note. It was lying just beneath one corner of Theodora's backpack, a folded sheet of paper with the words *Miss Oglethorpe* written on it.

"You had better read it," said Dr. Naga, handing it to her.

There were only a few lines, penned in a strong, clear script.

Dear Miss Oglethorpe,
We can only assume it is you who has brought the wyvern here, to a place of greater safety. For that, you have our

eternal gratitude. However, it is vital for the hatchling's sake as well as ours that we reunite this youngster with its mother without delay. Never fear, it is in good hands.

Your grateful servants,

Iain Merlin O'Shea, Ph.D., G.A.W.A.
Professor Emeritus, Harvard University

Gideon
Sorcerer Royal to the Court of His Highness,
Edward the Redheaded

At first Theodora stood dumbly holding the note in her hands, expecting it to vanish in a puff of smoke or turn into a frog and hop out of her hand. Wizards—not some lame, Wyvernkeeper's Circle wanna-bes, but the real thing. And right here in Cambridge. She felt a prickle run the length of her spine. It was as though she had written a letter to Queen Elizabeth I for history class, and the queen had written back, with a local postmark.

Then what the note actually said sank in, and Theodora sank to the floor with a groan. Now that the wyvern was gone she realized that, even more than walking into Traveler's Tales with the wyvernling on a leash and showing the Wyvernkeeper's Circle a thing or two, what she had really wanted was to be able to show it to her father so they could describe it together and publish the paper in *Science* and get their pictures on the cover of *National Geographic.* Then old Silverfish would have to make her father a professor, maybe even the chairman of the department, and they wouldn't have to move to some other city hundreds of miles away and leave Milo and Val and Mikko behind.

She looked up at Dr. Naga.

"I know it must seem crazy, but it really *was* here," she said. "But why should you believe me?"

Dr. Naga smiled. "Theodora, my dear! Of course I believe you. Even if I had my doubts, this would have convinced me." She held out her hand, and Theodora saw in her outstretched palm something like a large sequin, winking purple-black.

"It was in the old baby buggy," said Dr. Naga, letting the wyvern scale fall into Theodora's hand.

Theodora held it for a moment, not daring to breathe, as though breathing might make it disappear. Time seemed to stand still as the late-afternoon light from the window glinted off the surface in little rainbows. After what seemed like an eternity but was really only about ten seconds, Theodora drew a deep breath and slowly let it out. Then she carefully put the scale away in the change pocket of her wallet.

"Come," said Dr. Naga, reaching down and hauling

Theodora to her feet. "Let us go and see what has happened to Mikko."

Merlin and Gideon were in the kitchen of the apartment, examining the hatchling. A thick towel had been spread out on the kitchen table, and on it lay the wyvern, listless and peevish—though not so listless that it couldn't hiss and snap at the wizards if they got too close.

Gideon paid no attention to the bites on his hands, too absorbed in his examination of the young wyvern. He grasped one of the creature's wings, stretching it to its full length, and risked another painful pinch from the sharp beak, checking to see if the hatchling still had her egg tooth.

"A female," he said, "and hatched not two days since. We will have to make a batch of dragon's milk."

"In my youth," said Merlin, "dragon's milk was the cure for a bad hangover. In college we favored a cocktail of cold beef broth, raw egg, and a belt or two of good rye whiskey. I don't suppose it is authentic? The actual recipe has not been passed down in the Guild, I'm afraid."

Gideon managed a smile. "The dragon's milk I know is quite different. I used to brew it for Wycca. She had been taken too soon from her own mother and was not able to thrive on buttermilk. I will need a copper vessel, a pint of mead, a nugget of amber, and some musk."

"Well, I think we can approximate all those things," said Merlin.

A few minutes later, after some rummaging in his bedroom and in the pantry, the elder wizard had assembled on the counter a bottle of beer, a plastic squeeze-bear full of honey, a pair of amber cuff links, and a bottle of Manly Musk aftershave. He produced the last item a bit sheepishly.

"A gift from my goddaughter. But it's got musk in it, and I can only assume the other ingredients have some nutritional value. And beer with honey is the closest thing I have to fermented honey wine, I'm afraid. Though I could call a medievalist I know over at M.I.T. He used to brew mead for his annual Midsummer's Eve frolic. Awful stuff."

"There is no time," said Gideon, pouring beer and honey into a copper saucepan. While the mixture was heating Merlin pried the amber nuggets from the metal part of the cuff links and spun the amber in the food processor until it was a fine powder. Gideon added a pinch of amber dust and a few drops of Manly Musk to the saucepan, tasting the brew from time to time by dipping his pinky into it.

"A clean linen rag," he said sharply, holding out his hand like a surgeon asking for a scalpel. Merlin opened a drawer and produced a linen dishtowel. Gideon soaked one corner in the beer-and-honey mixture. Grasping the wyvern firmly, he pinned it against his ribs with one arm while he pried open the creature's beak and squeezed in a few drops of the dragon's milk.

The wyvern swallowed, blinked, and spit.

Gideon tried again and again. In the end, he was soaked in the mixture and there was very little, if any, in the hatchling itself. Gideon flung down the linen rag and swore—a good, long, elaborate medieval curse that made Merlin blush.

Gideon looked up at his friend and smiled ruefully. "Forgive me. I forgot myself."

"Think nothing of it. You have enlarged my vocabulary, and I assure you, that's not easy to do."

They looked at the wyvern, which was glaring at them, its scales puffed out for effect and its beak agape, ready to hiss and snap. But the creature was so weak it could barely hold its head up.

"Why won't she take it?" Merlin asked.

"Because someone—Wycca, Kobold, persons unknown—has fed her something else since she hatched. And now she must have that, or nothing." Gideon ran a hand through his hair, making it stand on end, mad-scientist fashion. "And if we cannot find out what it is, she will soon starve, and we will be helpless to prevent it."

18

Pitfall

OUROBOROS FOUND IT very difficult to keep the skunk focused on their quest for chocolate. She was easily distracted by all kinds of smells that Ouroboros found distasteful, if not downright repulsive: sour, oozy, ripe, garbagey smells.

"Ugh! What on earth is *that?*" the snake asked.

They were in an alley behind a row of condominiums, and the skunk had disappeared headfirst into the first of six large green garbage bins.

"Take-out Chinese, I think," said the skunk, her voice muffled by the walls of the bin. "Sweet and sour pork, by the looks of it. And some kind of pizza that might be pepperoni. It's gotten a bit green around the edges."

"I'm sorry I asked," muttered Ouroboros, gagging. "Well, if there's no chocolate in there, perhaps we'd better move on." The two previous stops on the skunk's garbage route had not yielded much: a squashed cereal box with a few chocolate wyvern marshmallows inside and an empty plastic cup with a trace of chocolate pudding still clinging to the bottom.

"I didn't *say* there wasn't chocolate," said the skunk. There was a rustling of paper and the sound of soggy cardboard tearing as she dug her way to the bottom of the bin. "Here we are."

The skunk emerged from the bin clutching a fancy velvet candy box in her jaws. Inside on a nest of gold tissue paper were nine large chocolate truffles and the crumpled foil wrappers for three more.

"It's always the same with this bin," the skunk explained. "Chinese food and pizza, then chocolates, and then nothing but lettuce, lettuce, lettuce. Today's a chocolate day. Tomorrow it will be back to lettuce."

Ouroboros sampled the air over the truffles with his tongue. "These should be perfect. But we can't carry the whole box back."

But they did manage to carry back five: the skunk stuffed a truffle in each cheek and took a third gently between her sharp teeth; Ouroboros took one in each of his mouths. Then, skirting the edges of driveways and decks and slinking under fences and around parked cars, they began to make their way back to the Oglethorpes' toolshed.

On the way to Theodora's house Dr. Naga asked a lot of questions about the Mikko-that-wasn't, and Theodora answered them the best that she could, telling her about seeing Mikko like a double exposure with tiny, round doll's teeth, and the nail polish on the carpet, and the dishwashing soap in the apple juice, and all the other strange things.

"Now, this is very important, Dodo," said Dr. Naga, as she turned the car onto the Oglethorpes' street. "Are you ticklish?"

Theodora turned and stared. "Well, I'm kind of old for tickling, but I think so. I mean, I used to be, when I was little." There went her brain again, replaying a home video of Tickle the Dodo, the three of them on the living room rug, gasping for breath, Mom laughing so hard she was crying.

Dr. Naga took a hand off the steering wheel and gave Theodora a quick poke in the ribs. Theodora let out a loud whoop and jumped in her seat.

"Just checking. It might come in handy. Laughter is a powerful charm against demons."

They parked the ancient green car a few houses away.

"Can we get in through the back door without being seen?" asked Dr. Naga.

"Yes," said Theodora. "We just have to duck under the living room windows."

The back door was unlocked. Theodora went first, because she knew how to open the screen door without it squeaking.

The kitchen was empty, but there on the floor next to the kitchen table was the familiar battered suitcase with the orange QUARANTINE sticker that had not quite been peeled off.

Theodora let out a squeal and ran into the living room. Andy Oglethorpe was sitting on the couch, his left leg up on the coffee table in a cast covered with writing in English and Laotian. There was no sign of nail polish anywhere on the couch, and the trail of silver toe prints on the carpet had vanished. From down the hall came the sound of Mikko's television.

Theodora flung herself into her father's arms. "Daddy! When did you . . . ? What are you . . . ? What happened to your leg?"

Mr. Oglethorpe smiled a sheepish smile. "Can you believe the very first day in the jungle I fell into a pitfall trap? A compound fracture. I had to turn right around and head back to Vientiane to catch the first flight back to New York. I wasn't in the camp even twenty-four hours. I tried to call you from the airport, but no one answered." He looked over Theodora's shoulder and paused for a long moment, then smiled. "Who's this?"

Dr. Naga had followed Theodora into the living room, hanging back during the father-and-daughter reunion. Now she stepped forward and held out her hand.

"Please let me introduce myself: Madhavi Naga, but please call me Maddie. I am an old friend of Mikko's."

There was another pause, almost uncomfortably long, as Andy Oglethorpe looked at Dr. Naga, his head on one side. "You just missed her," said Mr. Oglethorpe. "She just ran to the store, but she should be back in a few minutes. Would you like to hold?"

"Yes, if it wouldn't be too great an imposition," said Dr. Naga. "I have come at your daughter's request because she was quite worried about Mikko."

"Really?" Mr. Oglethorpe furrowed his brow and looked at Theodora. "She seemed fine when I got home. But come to think of it, Dodo, she did mention that the two of you had had a fight. She was still pretty worked up about it. Something about an old card?"

Dr. Naga started to say something, but Theodora had already dashed to her room to get the wyvern trump. It certainly sounded as though Mikko was back to normal—even her dad would know the difference between the real Mikko and the imposter—but she couldn't take any chances. She would have to show him the card and tell him everything that had happened before Mikko had time to get back from the store. Otherwise they might not have another opportunity.

She retrieved it from the box of wyvernalia she had pushed to the back of her closet and was about to run back to her father with it when she realized it was only the copy she had made with her father's scanner. Mikko had taken back the real card when she had walked in on Theodora casting the spell. She probably would have taken it to her room, unless she had hidden it on her way to answer the door.

Of course. The linen closet. The hiding place Theodora supposedly didn't know about, on the top shelf behind the sewing basket.

As soon as she opened the door to the linen closet she could see a loop of brass chain dangling from the top shelf. As she reached up to snag it, she could hear the muffled sound of the television from behind Mikko's closed door. It was unusual for Mikko to leave the TV on, but it was more than just that. Theodora stood there a moment, her fingers closed around the loop of chain, trying to think what it could be.

Then she shook her head. It had just been a long day. Her brain wasn't just fried, it was (as Val liked to put it) Kentucky-deep-fried. Mikko had probably been watching an old movie in her room when her dad had walked in the door, and the surprise had shocked her back to normal. She'd probably run to the store to get ingredients for her special celebration guacamole.

Theodora tugged on the brass chain and caught the purse in her hands. The wyvern card was inside, back in its protective cardboard sandwich. She took it into the living room and handed it to her father, seeing too late the look on Dr. Naga's face and the way she shook her head very, very slightly.

The door to Mikko's room opened and Mikko came out, carrying Frankie, followed by Konrad Lambton. She looked at Theodora and Dr. Naga and then aimed a glance of suppressed fury at Kobold. He snapped his fingers in front of her mouth, and Mikko immediately stretched her jaws and grimaced with relief, but without saying anything. It seemed her sarcastic comments hadn't gone over well with Kobold and he had kept her quiet with a spell.

Mr. Lambton went over to the couch and held out his hand, and Andy Oglethorpe surrendered the card.

The instant that the card left his possession, Theodora's father slumped back against the couch. Streams of cold, black smoke issued from his nose and mouth, winding themselves into a column in the middle of the room. As the column of smoke grew more and more solid it turned greenish, and before their eyes it took on the form of a hideous demon, what you might get if you crossed an orangutan with a gigantic iguana: a scaled creature with pouchy, bloodshot eyes, a protruding jaw with a large, droopy mouth, and a reptilian fringe that ran down its spine and along its tail.

Fumbling in his haste, Konrad Lambton separated the cardboard and tape with trembling hands and revealed the wyvern trump.

At first she had been frozen in place, but now Theodora let out a scream and tried to go to her father's side. But the oran-iguan-utan, or whatever it was, grabbed her by both arms and held her back.

"Don't worry, Dodo," said Mikko quietly. "That . . . *creature* . . . was in me too. Your father will be okay, but he will wake up with a pretty terrible headache."

At that moment Mr. Oglethorpe murmured something, tried to lift his head, and let it fall back against the couch with a groan.

Konrad Lambton ignored them, staring down at the card he held in his hands.

Suddenly all the pieces clicked into place in Theodora's tired brain: the sound from behind Mikko's door hadn't been an old movie but the whoops and shrieks and braying laughter of a trashy talk show, the kind of TV Mikko would watch only if you tied her down and held her eyelids open with duct tape. And then there was her father. Why hadn't he asked right away where she'd been or why she was coming home so late with a stranger? And then all the strange pauses, and the way he said, "Would you like to hold?" instead of

"Would you like to wait?" as though he had been playing back phrases from an answering machine.

Theodora felt sick in the pit of her stomach. It had been all wrong, but she had been so relieved to find her father at home, she hadn't seen the signs. And now the real wyvern card was in the hands of the creepy Mr. Lambton, whoever he really was.

Theodora thought of the note that had been left in the hideout. If there was a Sorcerer Royal running around Cambridge with a baby wyvern, it seemed there could be any number of wizards, witches, or warlocks looking for it, too.

Gideon and Merlin had not stopped to disguise themselves as animal control officers. There wasn't time. They scrambled out of a cab in front of the Oglethorpe house and ran straight to the shed in the backyard, the hatchling cradled in the younger wizard's arms.

They found Ouroboros waiting for them by the flowerpot, carefully guarding a pile of chocolate truffles as though they were a clutch of magic eggs he had laid himself. The snake needed only a second to take in the nearly lifeless hatchling and the wizards' grave expressions to realize how matters stood.

"It's chocolate. I was just about to roll these down into the burrow, but—"

Gideon didn't wait to hear more. He sat down on the

ground, forced open the hatchling's beak, and stuffed a truffle down as far as it would go. The wyvern gagged, struggled, and swallowed. Then it was still.

They all held their breath, waiting. A whole minute passed, and there was no movement from the hatchling, not a flicker. Gideon sat disbelieving, staring at the limp creature in his lap. At last he lifted it gently, as if to set it on the ground, when Merlin whispered, "Wait!"

The hatchling's eyelids fluttered and opened, then it opened its beak wide and loudly demanded another truffle. Gideon's shoulders sagged in relief, while Merlin gave a whoop of glee and began to do a tarantella of joy around the flowerpot, narrowly missing Ouroborous's tail in his abandon.

The hatchling's hungry cry grew louder. "Just one more," said Gideon. "We'll have to give the rest to Wycca."

"That's what I was trying to tell you," said Ouroboros. "I went down into the burrow to check on her and to give her a truffle. But she's gone."

19

In Kobold's Grip

"GONE!" SAID MERLIN.

"I'm afraid so," replied Ouroboros.

Gideon said nothing, just sat staring at the hatchling in his lap for a long moment. Then he reached into the pocket of his shirt and took out the fountain pen that held Ignus. He uncapped the pen and watched the intelligent Fire flow from the nib in a thin stream, forming an amorphous cloud about eight inches off the ground.

"Orb," he commanded, and the Fire obediently formed a hollow blue sphere, something like a soap bubble the size of a soccer ball, with silver electric sparks zooming over its surface with a static crackle.

Gideon lifted the hatchling and carefully placed it inside the bubble; the wyvern and the wizard's hands passed easily through the surface of the orb without popping it, though it did quiver and jiggle like Jell-O. The hatchling seemed a little startled at first, and then content, as though back inside the safety of its egg.

The younger wizard then spoke some phrases in Wizard's Latin, a spell of protection against mischief and worse, stitched neatly to another spell, for lightness, and when he was done the sphere with its hatchling cargo began to rise like a hot air balloon, until it was high among the branches of the copper beech tree.

It was still visible as an electric blue bubble of fire, so Gideon softly sent another spell up into the branches of the tree, and the bubble that was Ignus began to take on the color and the texture of the leaves until it was almost impossible to pick it out, even when you knew it was there, just a few yards overhead.

"Very nice," murmured Merlin. "Very nice indeed. You'll have to tell me exactly how you modified the incantation to get that shading on the leaves. But right now we have some demons to deal with."

Gideon's mouth twitched in a grimace. "Yes." He held out his arm, and Ouroboros coiled himself around his master's bicep, assuming his customary position for battle with demons. The younger wizard stood for a moment, with his eyes shut and his fingers closed around his owl pendant. Then he took a deep breath, opened his eyes, and looked at Merlin.

"I am ready."

As soon as he had the wyvern card, Mr. Lambton had gone into his briefcase and taken out an old book, its tattered pages neatly rebound in plain green cloth, and retired to the study with the book and the wyvern card and Mr. Oglethorpe's bottle of old Scotch whiskey.

This left the captives lined up on the sofa under the mournful gaze of the oran-iguan-utan. Andy Oglethorpe was still passed out, sleeping off the combined effects of jet lag and demonic possession, while Theodora sat between Mikko and Dr. Naga.

The demon was very interested in the pictures of Theodora and her father that were lined up on the mantelpiece. Noticing a smaller picture hidden behind the rest, the oran-iguan-utan picked it up and looked at it intently. It was a faded snapshot in a homemade Popsicle-stick frame, showing a woman in cutoff jeans and a T-shirt, with her hair pulled back under a bandana, kneeling by the base of a cliff. She was laughing, brandishing a pickax in one hand and a rubber chicken in the other.

"Who is this woman?" the demon asked. It didn't

speak in the croaky voice you might have expected from so ugly a creature, but in a higher, huskier pitch, like a glamorous actress suffering from laryngitis. Theodora wondered if it was the voice of Ms. Worm, but thinking back to Giles and Moira's bookshop, she couldn't remember Ms. Worm saying anything. The Mikko-that-wasn't had always used Mikko's voice.

"Who is this woman?" the demon said again, making Theodora jump.

Around the lump that had formed in her throat, Theodora said, "It's my mother."

The demon seemed to ponder this a moment, then it spoke again. "Where is she?"

"She died," Theodora said quietly. Mikko's hand reached for hers and gave it a squeeze.

The demon held the fragile frame—Popsicle sticks glued crookedly together, decorated with sequins and little plastic dinosaurs and hula girls and inscribed TO MOM, LOVE DODO—then carefully replaced it. The reptilian paws were more dexterous than they looked; the oran-iguan-utan was able to return the photo to its spot without knocking over any of the other photos.

It turned its pouchy, bloodshot gaze on Theodora and asked in its husky voice, "Why haven't you replaced her?"

Theodora shook her head. "You don't just replace someone you love. Even if you could."

The demon seemed to puzzle over this for a moment. Then it took a deep breath, and when it breathed out it was, briefly, Theodora's mother as she was in the photo: younger than Theodora remembered her, before she had gotten sick, before she had had Theodora, even before she and Daddy had gotten married (it was that rubber chicken, Mom used to say, that made her fall in love with Dad).

Then the demon was before them again.

"You could if you wanted to. Febrys would take her place."

"Febrys?" said Dr. Naga. "Is that your name?"

The demon lowered its eyes as if bashful. The bloodshot eyes were fringed with suprisingly long lashes. "Febrys. Demon First Class. Summoned by Kobold and servant to him."

"And Kobold is Mr. Lambton, I presume?" said Mikko.

The demon nodded, darting an anxious glance in the direction of the study.

"And you would rather serve Theodora, and be her mother, than serve Kobold?" said Dr. Naga.

But before Febrys could reply Kobold emerged from the study. He carried the ancient book in one hand, using his index finger to hold his place. In his other hand he held the Black Wyvern card.

"I have had a most fruitful search of your Internet," he announced. "There is a Web site for the Guild of

Adepts, where I am honored to see I am ranked high on the list of 'Most Wanted.' And the link to the list of banned spells has proved an invaluable shortcut."

Indeed, Kobold had discovered a way to enhance the power of the card using one of the banned spells. Now he no longer needed Gideon's wyvern in order to enact his revenge. He could simply shape the spell and send it out in search of his half brother. But first he would need to test it on someone. His gaze roamed thoughtfully over the row of captives seated on the sofa.

But Kobold had been pacing while he thought all this, and his path had brought him perilously close to the end of the sofa where Mikko sat with Frankie in her lap. As the wizard passed by the old white cat leaned out of Mikko's arms and bit him.

With a loud curse (which would have burned Theodora's ears, if it hadn't been hollered in medieval French), Kobold recited a string of strange words and drew a sign in the air. Instantly, Frankie shot out of Mikko's arms and flew around the room, spinning and tumbling as though in the grip of a small tornado. The big white cat came to a rough landing on the ceiling, where he remained stuck fast, like a fly on flypaper, trying in vain to lift his paws and yowling pitifully.

Theodora lost her temper. Before Mikko could stop her she had leaped up from the sofa and had fallen on Mr. Lambton, punching and kicking him as hard as she could and letting loose a stream of bad language in modern English. It was a good thing her father couldn't hear her. But at last she ran out of swearwords.

"He's just a poor old cat!" she said, gasping for air. "What did he ever do to you?"

These words were no sooner out of her mouth than Theodora felt a strange sensation, exactly as if a cold, invisible hand had reached through her skull, behind her eyes, and begun rummaging around in her mind. Memories spun through her brain in rapid succession: holidays past, days at the beach, her mom teaching her to ride her first two-wheeler, the time she fell out of the thinking tree and broke her collarbone, dancing with her dad at Aunt Jane's wedding . . .

Then the invisible hand found the memory it wanted and squeezed down hard, so that Theodora squealed in pain.

It was the last minute of the last hour of that last day; her mother, shrunken and weak and pale, was lying on the hospital cot in their living room, with Gran and Aunt Jane and Dad and Theodora gathered around.

Theodora realized that her memory wasn't going to suddenly change channels, the way it usually did. It was going to stay tuned to this memory, of all memories, as long as the invisible hand was squeezing hard on her mind.

Then, just as she was starting to panic, it was over. As the pain receded she realized that Mr. Lambton/

Kobold was looking down at her, gray-faced, beads of sweat standing out on his forehead. Going into her memory like that must have taken an incredible effort.

But the wizard was only pausing to gather his strength. The next moment the squeeze on her memory returned, twice as strong as before. Now, instead of being in her mind's eye, the memory was all around her, like a virtual-reality game. She could still see Dr. Naga and Mikko and her father on the couch, but their bodies were misty, like a cheap hologram. As they faded, the figures in the memory—her mother and Gran and Aunt Jane and her dad the way he had looked four years ago—grew more and more solid.

Theodora could feel the tears welling up inside her eyes, but in the grip of the spell she couldn't cry them. She felt a hand slip into hers and give it a squeeze, and she realized it was the scaly paw of the demon.

"Stop," Febrys hissed. Then the wizard muttered something in a strange language, and the demon gasped and began to whimper. Stubbornly, it kept its grip on Theodora's hand. But the figures on the sofa were getting fainter and the figures from her memory growing darker and more vivid and more real. Theodora knew somehow that if the figures on the sofa faded away entirely, she might not be able to get them back—or get back to *them.* Theodora was no longer sure whether she herself was still real, still Here and Now.

But now a new voice cut through the spell, uttering cool, silvery words in a calm tone. As they fell upon Theodora's ears the words sliced through the dark spell, and the scene of her mother's death fell away in long curls, like strips of wallpaper peeling away from the walls. Underneath was the actual room, with her father and Dr. Naga and Mikko on the couch, solid and warm and real.

Standing next to Theodora was a man she had never seen before. He had curly, mouse-brown hair and kind, gray eyes. She would have thought he was younger than her dad, the age of his grad students, maybe, except for those eyes. They held all the wisdom of a very old man.

Despite his outfit—a softball shirt with WORCESTER WIZARDS embroidered on the back—she knew at once that he must be one of the men who had left the note at the hideout.

This all went through her mind in no more than a second, the time it took for Gideon to step up to Kobold and seize the wyvern card. They each held on to it in a silent struggle, their hands trembling, as though they held a live electric wire. Looking at them, Theodora knew there was no danger of them tearing the card. It was stronger than either wizard or both together.

20

Where's Wycca?

IN THE OLD-FASHIONED comics and cartoons of Theodora's father's childhood, wizards wore long, purple robes with trailing sleeves and tall, conical hats spangled with stars, and they worked their magic by waving a wand. The wizards of Theodora's time—creations of video games and the movies and computer-enhanced special effects—were nothing so lame. These wizards had traded in their wands for an arsenal of death-dealing crystal daggers and flamethrowing staffs capable of reducing opponents to cinders or razing a castle in the blink of an eye. The sorcerers of *Wizards &*

Wyverns were fine masculine specimens, attired in tight-fitting costumes that showed rippling muscle to advantage, their manly grimaces and knowing smirks revealing flawless white teeth that had known all the benefits of twenty-first-century orthodontics (a head full of sound, unstained, straight teeth was almost as rare in the thirteenth century as a casket of myrrh or a sack of gold).

But now that there were two real, live wizards battling it out in the middle of her living room, Theodora discovered that reality was radically different from either imagining. Struggling silently for possession of the wyvern card, the two sorcerers presented an unlikely picture: Kobold in an expensive suit of Italian silk, Gideon in faded jeans, a softball shirt, and red high-tops. And they were armed not with quicksilver arrows or fireballs of supernatural lightning, but with words. Afterward Theodora was never able to recall exactly how the spells went—hardly surprising, as some of them were in Wizard's Latin, some in medieval French, and the rest in an obscure magical dialect still spoken in the Cantabrian Mountains of Spain. Thus the incantations below have all been spelled as they sounded to Theodora's ears.

"Limericks and lightning, locksmiths and lemurs!" Kobold muttered through clenched teeth. He had possession of only half the wyvern card, which seemed to rob the words of half their intended effect. The floor beneath Gideon opened up, as if to swallow him, but he sank through the carpet and floorboards only as far as his knees, never losing his grip on the wyvern trump and dragging Kobold down to the floor with him.

Theodora realized there was someone standing at her side and turned to find a stout professorly gentleman, looking a little disheveled in his shirtsleeves and red suspenders and the trousers of a brown tweed suit. He dragged his attention from the struggle long enough to whisper in her ear, "Miss Oglethorpe? We meet under most extraordinary circumstances. Iain Merlin O'Shea, at your service."

Gideon had now parried Kobold's spell. Scrambling out of the hole, he uttered something that sounded like, "Caravans and caramels, caraway and carousels," which caused the gray silk suit to turn into a coat of a hundred sleek gray moles with pink, star-shaped noses. This was an uncomfortable garment—hot, heavy, squirmy, and smelling like the small mammal house at the zoo—but Kobold dared not remove it, not knowing what the spell might have done to his silk boxer shorts.

"Can't you stop them?" Theodora said to Professor O'Shea.

Merlin shook his head. "I'm afraid Guild regulations limit me to the role of a 'second' in a duel: to make sure they fight fairly and, if necessary, to render first aid."

Kobold was slowly losing his grip on the card; the suit of living moles seemed to itch something fierce. But he managed to get off another spell, gasping out, "Gillyflower, gerrymander, gyroscope!"

The two-headed snake that was coiled around Gideon's arm suddenly grew to the proportions of an anaconda, threatening to suffocate the wizard in its coils. Gideon was still holding on to a corner of the wyvern trump with one hand, but his other hand was pinned against his side. His chest was so constricted by the snake that he couldn't draw enough breath to utter a counterspell. At last, in desperation, he let go of the trump and sketched a magical sign in the air.

It took Kobold a second to realize that he had sole possession of the card. He rapidly started to recite the banned spell. But Gideon's spell had gotten there first. The words fell from Kobold's lips as a thick ooze of honey that collected in a sticky golden pool at his feet, then as a stream of honeybees that formed a buzzing mask over the wizard's face. They did not sting but settled thickly over the wizard's eyes and nose and mouth and ears, so that no part of his face was visible except the dimple in his chin.

Ouroboros had by now resumed his normal size, but Gideon had suffered a cracked rib and was having difficulty catching his breath. This allowed Kobold time to sketch a spell of his own in the air, instantly freezing the mask of bees so he could pry it off in one piece.

Now there was nothing to stop him. The words of

the banned spell were ugly; they started deep in the wizard's chest, and they had a sickening sound, something like a plugged drain emptying, but also like someone spitting something foul out of his mouth.

As Kobold recited the spell, a form began to take shape in the middle of the Oglethorpes' living room. At first it was a swirling, vague column of air, shimmering like a mirage on a hot highway. Then it was darker and murky, a slick of oil on dark water. Slowly, it became the form of a young girl, no more than sixteen, her hair disarrayed and her long dress torn. Summoned up by the dark spell, she was a patchwork of reflections and shadows, not solid, not real, but horribly there all the same. In life she had been very beautiful, but now her pale face and staring eyes were those of someone lost deep in a labyrinth of insanity.

Gideon stared at this vision and whispered a name: "Gwynlyn!"

The sight of her appeared to pain him, but at the same time he seemed unable to look away. The vision took a step closer to him, stretching out a hand. Somehow Theodora knew that if the wraith or ghost or whatever she was touched Gideon, he would become a wraith, too. Was this still fighting fair? She turned to Professor O'Shea.

"Can't you help him?"

Merlin was already fumbling in his pocket, and he

drew out a foil pouch that looked a lot like the silvery plastic packages of astronaut ice cream Theodora's dad always put in her Christmas stocking. On the outside of the pouch were printed the words, SPELL PATCH KIT. FOR EMERGENCY USE ONLY. STORE IN A COOL PLACE. Merlin tore open the mylar with his teeth, seemed to draw out something invisible, and snapped it toward Gideon with the same motion you would use to shake out a bedsheet over a bed. Instantly Gideon was covered with a humming, shimmering net of golden light, like a thousand fireflies caught in a gossamer web.

But Merlin shook his head. "That won't hold more than a few seconds. My dear Theodora," he said, taking her hand, "lend me your mind and follow me."

For some reason she knew just what he meant, and squeezing her eyes shut, Theodora took Merlin's hand and mentally leaped into the fray. "Wishing" is not really the word for what she was doing; it only began to hint at the mental exertion involved, a painful stretching of her thoughts that made her head feel as though it were about to split open. She did not hear Merlin's voice in her head, but as she felt her fingers interlace with his, she was suddenly filled with the knowledge of certain things: that she had not found the wyvern trump, but it had found her; that her choice to put on her mother's brooch had not been random; that she possessed something, a talent, a birthright, a

"Greenwoodness" she had inherited from her mother.

All of this came to Theodora with the sudden clarity of a window being thrown open in a dim room, but she had no time to focus on it. She set her new awareness aside and turned her mind to saving Gideon.

It was as if she had been plucked from her body and asked to walk. The part of her mind she was being asked to use was a part she had never known was there. Again, without hearing Merlin's voice or sensing his presence in her thoughts, she suddenly knew how to go forward, sending her mind, joined with the wizard's, toward the wraith.

All around them the air rippled and writhed with Kobold's banned spell. Theodora was lashed and buffeted about in a storm of fear and pain, and under the fear and pain she could make out the shape of other dark things: envy and jealousy and pride and murderous hate, and she was shocked to realize these dark things came not from Kobold but from Gideon. They swirled around her, given shape and substance, and she knew that they came from Merlin and even from herself, that the wraith had the power to unleash and turn against them their own darkest thoughts.

She felt that her mind would let go and she would be swept up in the tide, but she felt the steady pressure of Merlin's hand and knew that she had to "wish" harder, with all she had left. The pain of it made her shriek and she felt herself losing her grip on Merlin and knew that if she did, the evil in the room would win.

But just as the wraith's fingers were about to close around Gideon's arm, there was a loud animal cry and something sleek and dark shot across the room and leapt upon the thing that Kobold had summoned.

No one afterward was ever able to figure out exactly what direction Wycca had come from, or where in the Oglethorpes' house she had been hiding, but later Theodora did discover some deep wyvern footprints under the kitchen window of the house next door and a crumpled, dented baking pan that had once held a batch of Mr. Togglemeier's famous chocolate–macadamia nut brownies. The scent of cooling brownies and the urge to find her hatchling had both proven stronger than the pain of her broken leg, and once out of the burrow she had caught the faint but unmistakable scent of a wraith.

The wyvern, revived and only slightly favoring her injured leg, seized the wraith by one skeletal wrist and worried it with a doglike fervor that rattled the pictures on the mantelpiece.

But the wraith did not simply fade away in the face of this attack. The spell was too powerful for that. The shadow-Gwynlyn's face twisted from a noiseless scream into a grimace of mad rage, and in a blink she had changed into a hulking thing with many terrible black eyes, like a spider's, and a gaping maw, more horrible for being toothless.

The wyvern held fast with her beak, raking at the creature with her talons. It changed again, taking the form of a wailing baby with green changeling eyes, but still the wyvern held fast. Then the wraith split itself in two, and in two again, until there were a dozen small wraiths scattering across the carpet, taking refuge behind the sofa and under the coffee table.

That, of course, proved fatal. Wycca dispatched the wraithlings one by one, like so many dragon treats, with victorious cries and loud snaps of her beak.

Next the wyvern fell on Kobold, closing her beak around his calf and bringing the wizard to his knees. The wyvern card fluttered to the floor, and Merlin nimbly stepped up and retrieved it.

While Kobold winced and cursed in pain, Ouroboros coiled himself into two half hitches around the wizard's wrists, preventing him from sketching any diabolical signs in the air or casting any other spells.

There remained only the demon. The wyvern had turned to deal with the oran-iguan-utan, which shrank back with a whimper. But Theodora quickly stepped between them, spreading her arms out to shield the cowering oran-iguan-uitan.

"No," she said. "Not this one. This one is all right."

Febrys's lip trembled and her long lashes were damp with tears.

"Wycca, heel," said Gideon, and the wyvern sat back

on her haunches, beak agape and her bright eyes never leaving Kobold. As Gideon stepped up and slipped the golden bridle over her head, the creature accepted it without a struggle.

Theodora had completely forgotten about the adults on the sofa. She turned to find Mikko gaping in amazement, Dr. Naga looking interested but not really surprised, and her father awake and alert. His features displayed a mixture of wonder, disbelief, and excitement. He was muttering under his breath and writing rapidly on the back of an envelope he had grabbed from the pile of mail on the coffee table.

"A new branch between the primitive Archosaurs and the Pterosaurs? But a quadruped like *Coelurosauraus*—those wings are for flapping, not gliding. That beaklike jaw—almost ceratopsian. Not crocodilian skin, but scales—some of the pterosaurians had a furlike covering . . . I'd like to get those scales under a tunneling microscope." Then he smacked himself on the forehead. "But the darn thing is alive! It's alive, alive, alive . . . Andy, Andy, Andy, you gold-plated idiot, all you have to do is draw a little blood and sequence its DNA!"

Mr. Oglethorpe threw down his pen and gave a triumphant howl of glee. He kissed Dr. Naga, and then he kissed Mikko, and then he got all flustered and started babbling to Dr. Naga about the pelvic rotation of things that can fly.

Theodora hadn't seen her dad look this happy and excited about anything since before her mom got sick. She felt a surge of relief. This was it. Such an earth-shattering discovery would surely get him his tenure. The wyvern was going to make everything all right. They wouldn't have to move and leave Milo and Val and Mikko behind. And then maybe, just maybe . . .

But just then Theodora glanced at the wizards and felt her stomach do a little sickening flip-flop. Some people's hearts might "sink," but Theodora always felt disappointment right in the pit of her stomach.

"He can't have it, can he?" she asked, by which she meant that Mr. Oglethorpe wouldn't be allowed to remember the wyvern, let alone measure it and examine it and analyze its DNA and write it all up as a cover article for *Science.*

Gideon smiled sadly and shook his head. "It would not be wise."

Merlin put a comforting hand on Theodora's shoulder. "Let us clean up here"—he indicated the trussed and sullen form of Kobold with a jerk of his head—"and reunite poor Wycca here with her baby. Then we will don our thinking caps and come up with a plan. Do you think"—and he turned here to Mikko—"you could provide us with liquid refreshment in some form? Spellcasting is such thirsty work."

21

Gwynlyn's Isle

IT WAS LATE August, and the Oglethorpe household had settled into its old routine, with some changes. While the wizards had not allowed Mr. Oglethorpe to remember the wyvern, it so happened that the fragments of a strange egg had been found in an abandoned peregrine falcon's nest in the Customs House tower overlooking Boston Harbor.

The fragments had been sent to Andy Oglethorpe's lab for analysis and identification, and it seemed that his paper on the egg and on a strange scale found with it was likely to be accepted for publication in *Science.* The

Silverfish was looking favorably on Mr. Oglethorpe's application for tenure, and Madeleine Silverfern had even invited Theodora to a skating party for her twelfth birthday. She had turned out to be much less stuck-up than you would have expected, though when Mikko had suggested they might invite Madeleine over, Theodora's dad had to ask his daughter not to make retching noises at the dinner table.

Mikko's mind had also been wiped clean of any memory of the summer's more remarkable events, though Theodora did catch her in the pantry once, holding a can of anchovies in one hand and a bag of mini-marshmallows in the other, a puzzled expression on her face. Then she had come to with a sneeze and gone on taking an inventory of her vast spice collection in preparation for the Oglethorpes' end-of-summer party and Ping-Pong play-offs.

This had been an annual event before Theodora's mother died, and when her dad had suggested it was time they had another party, it had been Theodora's own idea that it should be an Indonesian rijstafel with a vast platter of rice and about a hundred little bowls of things to put on it.

Milo and Valerie came to the party, looking very different after their summer away. Valerie was now wearing a bra (and very self-consciously, too), and Milo was so tan and tall from his summer on the ranch that he was barely recognizable. Theodora caught Valerie staring at him once or twice in a way that gave her a stab of something—not jealousy, really, but a feeling that somehow things weren't going to be the same in sixth grade.

The friends took their bowls of fried bananas and ice cream out into the yard to watch the first bats. The sound of music and grown-up chatter and laughter filtered out to them, and light from the house fell in long oblongs on the darkening lawn. After abandoning a halfhearted game of Ping-Pong, they all lay on the grass, talking about the summer.

"But what about you?" said Milo at last.

"Yeah," said Valerie, "what did you do with your dad away?"

"Oh, you know," said Theodora, tying a knot in a blade of grass. "I hung out with Mikko. We went to the library and the pond. It was pretty boring."

Valerie lay back on the grass with a small smile. She knew Theodora was holding something back, and she vowed to get it out of her, sometime when Milo wasn't around.

The next day was Theodora's twelfth birthday, and she tried to contain her disappointment when she opened the present from her dad: the director's cut DVD of *Wizards & Wyverns* (with nine minutes of new footage) and the GameBot cartridge for *Sibyls & Sorcerers,* the sequel to *Orcs & Omens.* A few months ago she would have fallen on him, shrieking her joy and everlasting gratitude, but now all she could summon up was a stiff smile and the kind of thanks you give the great-aunt who always gives you days-of-the-week underwear.

"I know," her dad said. "You're over all that wyvern stuff, but I reserved a copy on-line before I left for Laos to be sure I'd have it for your birthday. But I have something else I think you'll like better." Now he took something small and blue out of his pocket and held it out to her.

Theodora took it in her hands without understanding.

"It's Mom's passport," she said dully.

"Yes. I want you to have that until we can get you one of your own," her father said. "The next time I go out into the field, you're coming with me. Mikko and I think you're ready."

Theodora dropped the passport and hugged her dad and cried, and he hugged her back and cried, and even Mikko, who was in the kitchen and not cutting an onion, had to wipe her eyes on a kitchen towel.

It was only later, staring at the picture of her mother on the first page of the passport, that it occurred to Theodora her father had said "Mikko and I." She would have to work up the nerve to ask him what he meant. But not right now.

—⁂—

The following week there was a small gathering, attended only by Gideon, Merlin, Dr. Naga, and the honoree herself, Theodora, who was supposedly at Dr. Naga's house for a painting lesson. In Dr. Naga's living room, Merlin very solemnly presented to Theodora her very own official owl-and-crystal-ball pendant, with a clip suitable for attaching it to her backpack.

"But I didn't do anything," Theodora protested, as Merlin helped attach it to the metal ring on her backpack.

Gideon smiled at her. "But you did more than you know. You helped us find the hatchling, and without your aid in the delving, we would not have prevailed against the wraith."

"Is that what it's called? Delving?"

"That's one word for it, yes," said Merlin. "Nothing really precise in modern English, alas. The elves, now—they distinguish among dozens of varieties of delving. A remarkable language, Elvish."

There was also a handwritten citation for valor, on behalf of the North American Synod of the Guild for Adepts in the Wizardly Arts.

"The parchment copy will follow in four to six weeks," Merlin explained. "They're a little backed up, not because there are so many acts of valor waiting to be commended, but because the parchment citation has to be written out in salamander's blood. Since they're an endangered species, we have to wait for the salamanders to donate enough blood."

"Donate?" said Theodora.

"Yes. Through the Purple Cross."

Afterward there were speeches and toasts with glasses of limeade. It seemed a shame that Mikko couldn't be there—seeing all she'd done to restore the wyvern trump—but Theodora understood why Merlin, Gideon, and Dr. Naga had jointly decided to spare her and Mr. Oglethorpe any memory of Kobold and Febrys and the rest. Dr. Naga, it turned out, was not a member of G.A.W.A., but of a much older sorority with headquarters in Bangalore, India, and branches throughout India and Nepal.

Gideon and Wycca were going back through the bolt-hole to the thirteenth century. Well, not *the* bolt-hole—not the one that led from the castle's melon patch to the dance floor of the Club Golgotha in Central Square, but a different one. While bolt-holes going from Thens forward to Now were notoriously unstable, a nineteenth-century G.A.W.A. engineering project had succeeded in stabilizing bolt-holes going from the Now backward to various Thens, so that they ran with the predictability of the London Underground. Though there were several of these improved bolt-holes in Boston itself (including one under third base in Fenway Park), Gideon and

Wycca would be departing from a bolt-hole in the back room of a Salem fudge shop.

But Vyrna, as Theodora had named the hatchling, would not be going back with them. She could not return to a Where and When without chocolate. It was possible for Wycca to recover from her addiction but not so her hatchling, who had never known any other form of sustenance. Therefore, Merlin was giving up his emeritus position at Harvard and his apartment in the Agassiz Arms and setting out for a new life. He would divide his year between a ramshackle castle on one of the more obscure of the Orkney Islands north of Scotland, where Vyrna could hide among the misty ruins, and a cocoa plantation on the eastern coast of Costa Rica, where she could easily pass as a fruit bat.

When Theodora had excused herself to go to the bathroom, Dr. Naga glanced from Gideon to Merlin and back again.

"Shall you tell her?"

Merlin considered this. "That she is the descendant of a sorcerer? Not yet, I think."

Gideon had spent some time studying the snapshot of Theodora's mother holding the rubber chicken, and he had finally asked Theodora whether she had any more photographs of her relatives on her mother's side of the family. Theodora had produced a photo album, and among the ancestral portraits Gideon spied one faded and curling photograph of a young woman getting off the boat at Ellis Island around 1900.

There was no doubt that it was Gwynlyn. Her father had sent her to a "distant isle" to recover from her madness, and what more distant isle could there be than Manhattan at the turn of the twentieth century? And the women on Mrs. Oglethorpe's side of the family had all undoubtedly had, each in her way, "a wonderful way with dragons," whether they were cast in bronze on vessels from an ancient Chinese tomb, collected as fairy tales with a tape recorder by cottage hearthsides in Wales, or pried as "pterodactyls" from the limestone of a quarry in Germany.

"I will keep an eye on her," said Dr. Naga. "There will be time enough to tell her."

When Theodora came back from the bathroom, she gave the wizards her going-away presents, which had taken a lot of thought and had seriously depleted her savings account. For Gideon there was a silver Thinsulate vest, light and warm and waterproof, for his early morning practices with Wycca; for Ouroboros, a crazy drinking straw built for two, with as many loop-de-loops as a roller coaster; for Ignus, a pretty patterned glass bottle with a cork that had once held some fancy oil. And for Wycca, a bright orange Frisbee.

Gideon was quite moved. He and Merlin were going on to the fudge shop alone, with Wycca in a large crate marked CACAO/COCOA. So he had to say good-bye to Theodora on the steps of Dr. Naga's town house.

He looked into her eyes very solemnly, as if he saw something of Gwynlyn there, then laughed at himself and gave her a kiss on the forehead.

"Godspeed, Theodora Oglethorpe," he said. And then he was gone, wearing his new silver vest, with the rim of the orange Frisbee peeking out from the top of the knapsack as Dr. Naga's ancient green car careened down the narrow street, Merlin at the wheel, the large wooden crate tied precariously to its roof.

Dr. Naga consulted her watch, then slipped an arm around Theodora's shoulders, which were sagging very slightly.

"I promised Mikko I would have you ready to go home by four. Not really worth going back up to the studio to finish your lesson, but we just have time to take Kip and Rudy to the park to chase tennis balls."

The wizards were in the back room of the fudge shop, Gideon cross-legged on an enormous sack of roasted almonds, Merlin trying to look dignified while perched on a fifty-gallon drum of maraschino cherries. They had hauled aside the iron lid, the size of a manhole cover but covered in wizard's Latin. Now the bolt-hole shimmered in the middle of the concrete floor, awaiting them. In her cocoa crate, Wycca was napping.

"Merlin," Gideon said, "before I return to my own When and Where, there is something I have to tell you."

Merlin looked interested, but not surprised. "I think I know what it is," he said, "because I felt it too, during the delving. Go on."

"What Kobold did, he did not do for love or madness or revenge. Though perhaps he believed it, and we were meant to believe it too." Gideon toyed with the zipper on his new silver vest. "I could not prove it, I cannot say how I know it, but I would swear it was done at someone else's bidding. Something else was the prize—not Wycca, not her hatchling, not my destruction. If the wraith had seized me after all, what would have been my fate? Perhaps I was to be used, as it seems Kobold has been used. But to what end?"

Merlin shook his head. "A greater prize."

"But what?"

Merlin let his gaze roam around the storeroom, his eyes sparkling behind his spectacles. "Think about it, my friend. What is a greater prize even than Wild Magic? Controlling not bolt-holes, not mere Wheres and Whens, but a gateway to Never-Was. In the last twenty years explorers have found vents at the bottom of the sea, where molten rock flows up from the middle of the earth, like the old elvish legend that the center of the world is molten gold. Curious creatures live at those seeps, strange beyond our imagining. Some wizards have theorized there are seeps that let magic through, and strange things are drawn to those rips in the ordinary."

Gideon shivered. *"Magicus invertus?"* he said. This was the fouled magic he kept in a bottle tied with elvish harp strings, in a charmed iron box.

Merlin nodded, and consulted his watch. "I hope I am wrong. Time will tell. And speaking of time, my friend, it is time you were on your way. Try to send me a letter, now and then, by way of the melon patch. Dr. Naga will check every fourth Tuesday, and get word to me."

Gideon nodded, and checked for Ouroboros around his arm and Ignus in the flask in his pocket. Then he knelt to remove Wycca from the crate. She squawked in protest, opened her catlike eyes and blinked at him sleepily. "Come on," he muttered, as he slipped on her bridle, "there is a saucer of buttermilk for you on the other side." He clipped on the moonlight rope and wound the other end firmly around his waist, charming the knot. Then he stood and offered Merlin his hand.

"Fare thee well, friend."

Merlin returned the grasp and, affecting a thick brogue, recited the ancient Irish wizard's blessing, "May the moon rise up to meet you, and the wind be at your bidding."

With a cluck to the wyvern, Gideon stepped forward into the circle and they were gone.

And what became of Kobold and Febrys? The Guild decreed that, for the utterance of banned spells and general behavior unbecoming to a member of the brotherhood of sorcery (whether a member of good standing in G.A.W.A. or not), Kobold should undergo a Great Demotion, a procedure something between disbarring an attorney from the practice of law and declawing a cat. This left him with only the meekest of powers, but still powers enough to cause mischief in the halls of power in Washington, or on the selling floor of Wall Street. So Kobold, now in the persona of Konnie Lamb, was exiled to Hollywood to ply his talents among the other wizards of special effects. If you watch the credits of the next *Wizards & Wyverns* movie, you might see his name among the dozens scrolling by.

Febrys did not return through the bolt-hole. Gideon and Merlin were unable to grant her dearest wish, to become a human woman, but she now possessed too much heart to find work as a Demon First Class. After some thought the two wizards brought her to the Public Garden, and, under the cover of darkness, bestowed on her a new form. Ever afterward when Theodora went to the Public Garden, she was careful to seek out one particular swan—usually found squishing its webbed feet contentedly in the muck—and feed it marshmallows.